The Effect of Gun Control on African Americans

FREEDOM *is* DANGEROUS

JOSEPH C. KERR

Freedom is Dangerous
Copyright © 2025 by Joseph C. Kerr

Back Cover Photograph: Janet Sheard
Front Cover Photograph: Joseph C. Kerr
Inside Graphic: Joseph C. Kerr

Library of Congress Control Number: 2025905339

ISBN
978-1-964488-66-0 (Paperback)
978-1-964488-67-7 (eBook)
978-1-964488-65-3 (Hardcover)

Table of Contents

Introduction

Any tool humans make can be used as a weapon. The development of weapons is one the most profitable enterprises on earth. African Americans don't produce any of them. Neither do we control any of the products or services related to them. All the firearms purchased by African Americans, the US military, law enforcement agencies, and law-abiding citizens, or confiscated in connected with crime, surrendered during gun buyback programs, and restricted from you by law are manufactured outside of African American communities, control, and benefit.

I'm American. That word entitles me to all the rights of the Constitution. I identify myself as American and it says that on my passport. I'm also a Negro. That word gives me connection with all other people identified as Negroes on the planet. I'm also an African American, or should I say that is my current politically correct, superficial, socially acceptable racial identification based on my physical appearance, blood connection and available paper trail. That identification gives me connection to all Africans brought to America as slaves and to people who immigrate here from around the world to live free. I may also be identified as Black, Colored, Nigger or other stereotypical branding depending on who is doing the identifying. My DNA carries a significant amount of African, European, and human genetic markers unique to American descendants of slaves, slave owners and other people living in North America in the past five hundred years. I don't expect my friends or family to call me anything other than my name, except in anger or as a term of endearment: "You my Nigga" vs "Fuck you, nigga". I don't know what to expect from individuals that I don't know. America has never been a safe place for defenseless people, but especially for people who look like me. The funny thing is that if you were looking at me, I wouldn't have to tell you my inclusive identity group or my pronoun, you will assign these things to me in your own mind and I will not insist on you, calling me anything.

African Americans currently do not manufacture any firearms in America. No African American currently holds a federal license to import, manufacture or distribute firearms in the US. That means no matter what restrictions the government imposes regarding gun control, unless African American begin to manufacture firearms, our access to these tools for self-defense will remain limited and mostly illegal. American universities graduate African American engineers, scientist, business professionals, lawyers, and great thinkers every year. The US military is full of African American engineers, business professionals, lawyers and doctors, combat specialist. Yet African Americans are not involved in one of the most profitable businesses in the world, except as employees, consumers, and victims of illegal use of these products. This is the time and opportunity for African Americans to design and manufacture one of America's leading products for domestic sales and foreign export. Manufacturing small arms is and remains a cottage industry institution. It is a small business anchor in many rural communities. It's labor intensive, requiring attention to detail, reliable quality, and dedication to the economic success of the entire population. Right now, small independent firearm manufacturers are causing the industry's leading manufacturers to rethink their business models. The US government today is purchasing the new standard issue sidearm from a foreign, firearms manufacture while Americans are in need of economic opportunities between wars.

Throughout these pages you will discover a variety of firearms and related products presented as challenges for our economic, civil, and physical survival. I am not an advocate for anyone to arm themselves for any reason. I am an advocate for fully participating in this American experiment. Ask Frederick Douglas

You are invited to discover a variety of self-defense related products which could be produced by African Americans nationwide today. Offered for your imagination a company called Niggas, Ltd. It is a community-based idea incubator and neighborhood collective manufacturer of firearms and self-defense products. Founded by Cole and Damascus Steal, a father and daughter team of divided Americans, Niggas, Ltd is a company where dedicated African American professionals are engaged in independent local product manufacturing to economically energize and stabilize their communities. It began as a viable form of reparations through, the use of civil instruments such as imminent domain for community benefit and small business loans to challenge African American graduates from the best universities in the world to stimulate local self-reliance and sustainability in our communities. African American military veterans who have bravely, lead our children into battle to protect American interest around the world are consulted throughout design and development of all products and are encouraged to join us when they separated from active service. Niggas Ltd is an inclusive collective of individuals interested in sustainable economic, civil, and social development for our challenging times. They intend to form collectives, co-operatives, and non-profits, without government assistance or influence, to develop, manufacture and distribute simple safe and affordable firearms and related products for personal protection and police/law enforcement service to turn the American dream into your imagination.

There are no statistical analyses, verified facts, or objective evidence offered regarding anything, or idea presented herein. I'm not presenting any profound knowledge to you. The use of derogatory, inflammatory, offensive, adult language and descriptions are intended as humor. This is a work of plausible reality fiction. Names, characters, businesses, places, people, events, locations, and incidents are either the products of the author's imagination or used in a fictitious satirical manner. Any resemblance to actual persons, living or dead, or actual events is purely coincidental. No disrespect intended to any person living or dead.

Millions of US citizens lawfully purchase and use firearms every day for millions of legal reasons. I hope to distract you from the entertainment of our government and media manufactured fear of these tools so essential to the concept of freedom. Our challenges as human beings moving forward in this time will be increasingly competitive and dangerously restrictive. If strong possibly offensive language disturbs your sensibilities, please give this book to someone for their consideration. Thank you.

If any of the issues described in this book resembles life for people where you live, regardless of your color, ethnicity, national origin, age, religion, political beliefs, sexual orientation, or social identification, you understand that we are forced to fight for rights already guaranteed to all citizens in accordance with the Constitution. This book is about the effects of "Gun Control" on Negros in the United States of America. Freedom is dangerous.

Challenge One

This is the first of many challenges presented to all African American engineers, manufactures, entertainers, celebrities, and entrepreneurs, to design, manufacture, and market affordable and concealable handguns for individual self-defense and law enforcement service. Niggas Ltd, is looking for qualified motivated individuals to participate in the development and manufacturing a two shot, pistol with an over/under barrel configuration, ambidextrous safety, light weight, concealable, affordable and recyclable. We need your passion for freedom and prosperity to make it happen.

Constructed from domestically sourced recycled steel and composite materials it will be cheap to own, easy to control, limited capacity, easy to get loaded, and lethal when discharged. They will be called: Niggas. They will be chambered for .22 Cal (The Little Nigga), 9mm (The Street Nigga), .357 to .50 Magnums (The Big Nigga), through the use of interchangeable barrels and modular frames. All Niggas will be affordable and easy to use. If your Nigga has a quick trigger, it can be adjusted with a screw. Use a little coin to tighten it up if it gets too loose.

Developing, producing, and selling Niggas will provide much needed jobs, social and economic stability for African American communities throughout the country, but especially in our inner cities where local manufacturing could halt the displacement of these people. Everybody will want to own a Nigga. When you have a Nigga with you, whether it's a Little Nigga or a Big Nigga, a Nigga by or on your side, and a Nigga in the house, Niggas will keep you and your family safe. But you don't want a Nigga in your face. Just seeing a Nigga is enough to deter most people from doing you harm. Warning: It may be illegal in some states for you to own or have a Nigga with you in public. Some states want to prohibit citizens from owning Niggas or any other firearm for self-defense or safety.

In the beginning

When the world was mostly tribes of people, everyone was expected to be armed to defend themselves and their territory from other people and dangerous animals. Very young humans were taught to make, use, and care for weapons for self-defense and survival. As civilization expanded, dominant groups of people began disarming weaker groups of people and crime against humanity began around the world. Rocks, spears, arrows, knives, dogs, and cameras are no match for guns. People who cannot or will not protect themselves will be mistreated by those seeking control. Throughout the history of humankind, people who have everything have attempted to control the people who have nothing. The founding fathers of the United States of America understood this and wrote into our foundation a method to prevent the disarming of any citizens by the government with few limitations.

So along comes, the American experiment, equal rights, equal opportunities, and equal protection for everyone. Let's ignore the brief incidences of genocide against the indigenous people of the west and that little slavery thing. It was so long ago, and America is still trying to be something different. Our natural defense against each other and other beings is the ability to make and use tools/weapons. Taking away a human being's ability to defend itself is like declawing a lion. It can still roar as it's being consumed by hyenas. Roaring is not self-defense.

The Right to Bear Arms

Freedom is dangerous. Freedom is not granted to you by the state you live in or the federal government. The Bill of Rights does not grant citizens any rights. It is the People's instructions to our elected government representatives, describing the conditions essential for people to live free. The physical act and responsibility of the individual to keep and bear arms is what makes America free and unique among global powers. No other superpower nation or government trusts its citizens this much. This responsibility is what guarantees all our other rights. If we allow any further infringement of the right of free people to bear arms, we can't expect to protect any of our other rights. It is the only right in the Bill of Rights that explicitly states that it shall not be infringed. There is not one word about hunting, sports, or safety in the Bill of Rights. Be leery of a government that disarms its law-abiding citizens for their own safety and protection.

At the time of the American Revolution the people were being physically and economically crushed by a financially insatiable and an incessantly oppressive government. The colonialists complained about the distribution of wealth from taxes and abuse of law enforcement. It was a time of great terror inflicted on people by competing governments for control of resources and people. Wealthy, powerful, individuals and organizations use deadly force to control the weak, needy, impoverished and enslaved. During this period of global expansion native peoples had only clubs, knives, arrows, spears and dogs, common tools for hunting and self-defense. Slaves had some access to farm tools, and these were no match for determined people with guns. Our nation was founded on the belief it was necessary that every able-bodied person except for Negroes, be armed for personal protection and to free themselves and their property from the government.

To all who believe the Bill of Rights is being misinterpreted regarding individual rights to keep and bear arms. The first part of the amendment addresses the establishment of militia. It is very specific regarding the need for a well-regulated militia. At that time, it meant that able-bodied citizens should consistently meet with their weapons to prepare for the defense of their families and homes independent of government support. The second part is also very specific. Only the People's right to keep and bear arms shall not be infringed. I can't find the section that states the People have no right as individuals to keep and bear arms. Or where it says each state shall create laws to restrict individual access to common arms. I can't find the paragraph stating that only police and state sponsored militia should be armed for the People's protection and safety. Or where it states that the police shall be armed greater than the People for the People's protection, the People shall only be allowed to possess state approved hunting style arms for legal civilian activities, the People shall not be armed in public except as privileged by government authorized license. That any firearm license issued is only valid in the state where it was issued. Each state and each subdivision of that state can create safety laws to infringe on this right of the People. The People must register their arms with the government for accountability, safety and crime reduction. Where does this amendment only approve arms for regulated hunting and sports? Can anyone point out any arms restrictions in the constitution to me? But every means of deception and restriction has been employed by federal, state and local governments to deny the People this fundamental right and protection as citizens. These limitations and restrictions have been written into state law by mystics and interpreted by magicians, we elected as our representatives for our safety, and no one feels safe.

It took a Civil War and two more amendments to clarify to our elected officials that African Americans are citizens by birth and blood. The 14th Amendment states that all persons born or naturalized in the United States, and subject to the jurisdiction thereof, are citizens of the United States and of the State wherein they reside. No State shall make or enforce any law which shall abridge the privileges or immunities of citizens of the United States; nor shall any State deprive any person of life, liberty, or property, without due process of law; nor deny to any person within its jurisdiction the equal protection of the laws.

We have become a nation of laws so complex that even the people who write them don't understand them. Law-abiding citizens agree to obey what they believe to be the law. Every time someone willfully breaks the law, new laws are imposed on everyone who obeyed the law. Today, we have so many new laws that no matter what you do, you're going to violate some of these laws. And this is how the state-sponsored legal robbery and criminalization of citizens begins and enforced by a self-serving financially insatiable government at the point of a gun. So, we know that new laws can't be the answer to what ails America. Ask Barack Obama. Simply being armed should never be a crime in this country unless a crime is being committed by the armed individuals. Firearms are the symbol of our American heritage and freedom. This idea is embodied in the statue of the Minute Man bearing his rifle prepared to confront tyranny. This is a right for US citizens, not everyone. Aliens should not be armed. This should be the rule for everyone, including persons who have paid their debt to society. This would free our courts and elected representatives to solve real problems for America.

Crime

Every time the media says a Black person was killed by a police officer; it makes me feel that the media believes that Americans are blind and stupid. They produce video images of the incidents, victims, and perpetrators. A picture is worth a thousand words, and it looks like police are killing a lot of Americans without judicial process. And when they report black on black crime, it looks to me like ordinary people killing each other out of nonsensical motivations and stupid reasons. The images are disproportional to the population and the truth.

We can't be free while living in fear of an ever increasingly oppressive, incompetent, and corrupt government, willful criminals, and greedy corporate empires. It's easy enough for African Americans and other clearly identifiable people to be singled out as the imaginary source of America's problems. But we all know that our frustration comes from being terrorized and traumatized into submission to the wealthy and powerful.

Remember it was the American people that rebelled against the English government and General Washington's army was initially a secret group of armed and willing civilians. African Americans should have an honest conversation with each other about gun control, law enforcement, and public safety. Why are we, African Americans so ideologically polarized about products and behavior that we don't control? We have allowed the government and media in blackface to speak for all of us through the voices of distraught victims of criminal atrocities, the eyes of law enforcement, agenda driven politicians and the media. We must realize that America has never been safe for us. Never! With all the law enforcement agencies, all the public surveillance, the proliferation of the new laws, and private prisons overcrowded with our children, crime where most African Americans live continues to escalate.

Why is crime so low in other communities? They don't have a lot of police resources, yet they have almost no crime. Except for the daily domestic disturbance, murder, rape, robbery, suicide, home invasion, prostitution, human trafficking, kidnapping, vandalism, drug lab, bomb making, traffic violations, and a variety of predatory frauds and extortions, other communities are virtually crime free. You see even they're not safe from each other either.

Isn't it amazing that while law enforcement officials claim to be outgunned by criminals, the criminals are not breaking into or attacking police facilities to take the guns, drugs, cars, and money at these defenseless facilities? Neither are the troubled youth perpetrators of murder and mayhem going down to the local police headquarters or television station to shoot up a building full of armed individuals.

In the US crime pays! We glorify and justify the perpetrators of crime at the expense of the victims. How much money did the government collect from you this past year for law enforcement? (Taxes, fees, citations...) Do you feel safer because of the police where you live? If you were the victim of violent crime, you might consider being armed. The police are armed and according to the police, so is everyone else. By now shouldn't we feel safe in our own neighborhoods? People who cannot protect themselves are subject to mistreatment by those who wish to do them harm. The response to crime can't always be passive or politically correct.

Should the US government run to the aid of defenseless people around the world? On moral grounds the answer is always yes. Economically it is great for business and bragging rights when you're on the right side of history, and no shame if you fail. We want people around the world to stand up for themselves, so we arm them. Before this war between the police and the people escalates any closer to turning the US into a total police state for our safety, every eligible citizen who chooses (with appropriate training), should consider being armed. Please don't confuse self-defense with taking the law in your own hands. You can't keep what you can't protect.

Intimidation and murder are crimes the police shouldn't be a part of. The tools used during a crime should not be confused with the choices or actions of the persons committing the crime. Blaming the tool for the work of the carpenter is what we are being asked to accept as a reasonable justification for us to surrender our rights. Are the police really better carpenters?

Why, are African Americans the most feared unarmed and defenseless people in America? Why do African Americans dread the police more than the criminals in their communities? Most African Americans live in areas where local laws prohibit law abiding citizens from being armed for any reason. While armed police and criminals in these areas use us as their inexhaustible source of funding and power. They say the money is power and they're both costing American citizens billions.

Why are the police chasing stolen cars and killing car thieves when you are required to have insurance? Why do you call the police when your car is stolen? They don't have a vested or financial interest in your insured personal property. In the process of the police pursuing your insured property they have racked up a lot of dead bodies, millions in property damage, and billions in civil settlements that we the taxpayers are responsible for paying. That new very expensive police special pursuit vehicle that was used as battering ram to stop your stolen insured personal vehicle was paid for by you. Most stolen vehicles are recovered within days without the need for armed intervention. The police know where stolen vehicles are taken and for what reason. So do the insurance companies, body shops, salvage yards, backyard mechanics, and people looking to cut repair costs. The only reason for a police officer to get involved with the loss of your private property is to keep the peace between involved parties or to save someone life. And that financial settlement from the city was paid by you. The city doesn't have any money of its own. Think about it.

Imagine driving from here to there and you're stopped by the police. The officer asked you to exit your vehicle for whatever reason. Out of civil obedience and belief that you haven't violated any laws, you inform the officer that you're armed and have a concealed carry license from your home state. The officer informs you that you're in a "gun free" state, and without incidence you surrender your firearm and yourself to the police like a good citizen. This is where policing for profit begins. They seize your weapon (retail value), impound your vehicle (resale value), cash bond (State mandated), and traffic citations for transporting a prohibited item. Attorney fees (going rate), court cost (they determine), and other related expenses and fees. If you plead not guilty, you may still be incarcerated in states with mandatory incarceration for firearm violations. Your employer will be notified, who may choose to terminate your employment even before guilt or innocence has been established. All for possessing a tool that no law enforcement officer or persons planning do you harm would leave home without. California has a mandatory ninety-day incarceration requirement for anyone carrying a weapon in public without a government issued permit. It's easy money for everyone but you.

Why are there so many variations in traffic and firearm laws from state to state if these laws are not just revenue generators? Is a person in a rural area more likely to be raped, robbed, murdered, or attacked by a vicious animal or dangerous human than an individual in urban areas? Is a police officer's life in more danger than yours because you are armed for self-defense just like the police officer? The police and the government want you to give them credit for crime reduction where you live. But you know the truth is that crime goes down where criminals can't afford to live. Not because of the police. Unfortunately, when the criminals can't afford it, neither can you.

Challenge Two

With the projected success of the Niggas brand firearms, Niggas Ltd. would like to invite you to invest in the development, marketing, and sales of our newest pistol, the Bitch. The Bitch will be marketed specifically to women. A two-shot pistol with an over/under barrel configuration, ambidextrous safety, light weight, concealable, and inexpensive. They will be constructed with locally sourced steel and recyclable composite materials, for frame, weight and size reduction! The Bitch, available in black, tan, or yellow frames with color matched hypoallergenic organic synthetic rubber grips (10% of sale revenue donated to victims of domestic violence, women shelter organizations) and the Pink Bitch: stainless steel with choice of pink or white imitation pearl grips on a composite white frame (10% of sale revenue donated to breast cancer research organizations). All Bitches will have the integrated intuitive lazar sight for improved accuracy.

Women are the most likely to be physically attacked on the street and in their homes. Handguns are the most versatile, concealable, and useful deterrent to violent attacks on women. Handguns are also easier to handle in the home resulting in less property and collateral damage than shotguns and rifles.

Historically handguns were designed for large masculine hands. They were heavy, awkward, bulky, and hard in small hands, requiring a two-hand grip for control. A smaller frame gives women a more natural grip and aim when defending themselves and their families.

Cheap to purchase, easy to control, limited capacity, easy to get loaded, and lethal when messed with. The Bitch chambered for .22 Cal long rifle including bird shot, .45 LC, or .410 gauge. This gives women options to satisfy their needs and situations. All Bitches will be affordable, easy to use, and low maintenance and self-lubricating. If your Bitch is quick to go off, like the other Niggas, they can be adjusted with a screw, use a little coin to tighten them up. You will feel safe and protected when you own a Bitch. A Bitch is more than capable of getting the message across to anyone infringing on your comfort zone. No one wants a Bitch in their face, but a Bitch can save your life. Remember to always be careful when handling a Bitch, because a loaded Bitch can kill you.

Negros in America

The history of Negros in America has been and continues to be repression, suppression, and incarceration in the land of the free. Prosperity is out of reach for most of us, according to the media. The absolute, majority of Africans arriving in the new world were not immigrants. We were brought here as slaves, free labor with no rights. With the signing of the 13th amendment, African Americans became emancipated property with no national origin, native language, customs, or rights. The US Constitution was the law, but most states still refused to recognize us as full US citizens even after the 14th amendment.

African Americans should never forget that the army, the police, the courts, and the banks have been used to suppress and control us since we arrived on this continent. We are the picture of what forced freedom looks like.

African Americans want the freedoms guaranteed to all citizens. You see, African Americans are happy people, easily distracted by shiny things. Our memory of the bad things that happened to us as individuals or as an identifiable ethnic group throughout American history has been almost washed away by the apparition of political power, the amnesia of consumerism, the hypnosis of entertainment, the illusion of technology, the desire for assimilation, the unfaltering belief in things we cannot see, and the fear of becoming victims of the law. We are American. Ask Frederick Douglas

Some level of citizen

This is about the Constitution as it applies to all US citizens since the end of the civil war when the United States was still a new country with liberty and justice for some. Prior to that, Negros, were considered subhuman commodities without any rights or legal recourse in the country we helped to create. The Emancipation Proclamation did very little to make Negros anything other than some level of citizen in most states. By virtue of social practice and law, equal to other Americans in no state. The 13th Amendment did not obliterate the institution of slavery. It changed the language we used to identify and control the underclass people in America. Throughout our history, states have been increasingly oppressive in their approach to curtailing our rights as they relate to self-determination and self-defense. The current gun control laws are designed to keep

US citizens from exercising basic rights of life, liberty, and the pursuit of happiness. Happiness, as in living without fear of our government or our neighbors!

The idea of armed Negros became especially troublesome right after the civil war. It was frightening to the good people of our mostly segregated nation. Discharged Negro veterans with newly acquired freedom, military skills, and battlefield successes were migrating into the western frontier regions of the country to begin new lives, expecting equal rights as full citizens. But America was having none of that.

Most veterans of the civil war were allowed to keep their small arms (pistols and rifles) issued to them by the military when the war was over. Others traded things or services for guns, found them and or stole them. Firearms were expensive to buy, and a good one could cost a month's earnings, and that didn't include the ammunition. However they were acquired, most people owned firearms, and everyone was expected to be armed, except for Negros. Guns were an instant equalizer and peace maker in the civilizing of the west.

Only Negros in uniform (soldiers and police), were allowed to carry firearms in public in most cities and towns. Even in uniform, Negro soldiers could be required to stow their firearms by order of their commanders when entering an area where armed Negros, were prohibited.

Many of these blatant infringements have been perpetrated through state government interpretation of the Constitution as it pertains to identifiable groups of people. The Black Laws or Black Codes, denial of voting rights, gerrymandering, and denial of judicial protection, have been written into law. Out of fear that Negros would demand equal rights by force, gun control laws were imposed nationwide. This is not to say that no other people were targeted for discrimination by way of individual state laws. But African Americans are the only US citizens emancipated from property (chattel slavery) to some level of citizenship. That gives us a unique status in the discussion of American freedom.

Yes, over time there were free Americans of African descent, coexisting with other Americans and some even had ownership papers for other African Americans. So, few African Americans could fit this new truth about our American heritage that it took Hollywood and the Public Broadcasting System to remind us of our contribution to our own subjugation. But the exclusion from the benefits of full citizenship applied to all Negros, whither slave or free. African Americans have been denied citizen's rights for so long that we don't believe we actually have any. Some people have even suggested that we are blessed to be in this country, as if we haven't contributed to America's existence, growth, and prosperity.

While African Americans are still being encouraged to pursue passive methods of achieving the full citizenship already guaranteed to everyone born in this country, all manner of violence is still being perpetrated against us nationwide by other citizens (including our people), and law enforcement agents of the government.

The history of how African Americans have been swindled, hypnotized, bullied, and legislated out of the right to armed self-defense should be an issue brought before the Supreme Court as a matter of life and death. America has never been a safe place for Negro people. The military, the police, and the courts have been used to intimidate, attack, murder, and control African Americans throughout American history. Even at the beginning of the 21st Century, African Americans are still being demonized, criminalized, marginalized and murdered in the popular culture and rendered helpless through the denial of our basic rights by state and local governments, while we get taxed at the same rate as everyone else.

Most African Americans don't understand the real dangers of our current gun control laws. The truth is not being told or heard. The debate made through the corporate news media and the halls of congress are only about controlling you. African Americans need to hear from legitimate sources of information other than the corporate news media sound-bite interviews with distraught victims of crimes, inept self-serving self-aggrandizing political figures, law enforcement agency spokespersons, polarizing religious zealots, corporate and social media influencer pundits. I grieve with the victims of crime for the stupidity of ending someone's life for non-sensical reasons and the trauma to our communities and country. But that's no reason to surrender my rights. Why aren't we hearing from our veterans who have stood bravely and served this country in armed conflicts when America's global interests have been threatened?

The problem for most minorities in America is that we keep forgetting that we, along with everyone else, are what's great about this country. We have allowed others to mute our voices and speak for us. Feminists, LGBTQ, people with disabilities, and failing corporations have all benefited as a result of following President Obama's instructions to stop asking for what's already yours and start demanding it. We helped organize these other groups, took to the streets, to the media, to the government, and the courts, and caused the government to enforce the laws pertaining to those causes. African Americans are still begging for simple equal rights and legal protection. We've been trying to live the American dream of assimilation, but where has that gotten us as a clearly identifiable group of dissimilar people?

African Americans have also given and continue to leave our blood on America's battlefields both foreign and domestic. We are battle weary, suffering severely from post-traumatic stress, attention deficit disorder, and a general malaise that conditions us accept abuse. But we are battled hardened on all fronts as we continue to fight and die for the rights of all Americans. It is time to demand the right to be armed and an end to qualified immunity for our paid protectors.

People from all over the world have migrated to this continent since the beginning, bringing with them their own customs, languages, and religions. This allowed most new Americans to maintain successful practices from their ancestral origins, including establishing social boundaries worth protecting. African Americans don't have any culture or language other than American. Most of African Americans ancestors arrived here as property and were forced to abandon traditions and adapt to the rules, customs, language, religions, and laws of this land.

The majority, of African Americans have never actually been permitted to exercises all, rights of US citizens. Especially the unimpeded right to defend yourself on the street or in the courts. And as US citizens and military members, African American have witnessed the mistreatment of defenseless people around the world, while we continuing to suffer at home from individual state-imposed oppression.

African Americans don't run away when asked to fight for America. So why should we have to hide in our homes when a war is being waged all around us in our community? Our children have become the soldiers and the collateral damage of warring factions of armed domestic criminals and armed law enforcement agencies battling for resources and control of our communities. We have been rendered helpless as a result of state and local governments' manipulation of the constitution. Inside the borders of the United States of America, no one has ever been safe from the environment, man or beasts. African Americans just stand out. And if we are going to ever be safe here, we must be able to protect and defend ourselves. My body, my choice.

Here's what I know

African Americans do not manufacture any firearms in the USA. No African American holds a federal license to manufacture or sell firearms in the USA. That means, no matter what restrictions the government puts in place regarding gun control, African Americans access to firearms will remain limited, expensive, and mostly illegal. American universities graduate African American engineers and scientists every year. The US military is full of them, and they can't figure out how to make a simple handgun after they leave the service. Some education system isn't it!

There are African American billionaires, but we don't manufacture any weapons. We own entertainment and sports franchises producing, promoting athletes, artists and entertainers known around the world. We have shipping and construction companies. We graduate doctors, scientists, engineers, teachers, reporters, lawyers, artists and great thinkers from the best universities in the world. We have been commanders of the most powerful military force ever known, and buried with metals of honor, but we don't manufacture weapons. Among us are countless philosophers, entrepreneurs, artists, activists, preachers, neighbors, prisoners, police officers, teachers and politicians, but we do not manufacture weapons! We have given our lives, money, and votes to support and protect America's interests around the world, but we don't manufacture any weapons. From the beginning, we have been an indispensable partner to America's wealth and prosperity, but we don't control the manufacturing or profits of any weapons made anywhere. We don't even talk about African Americans making weapons. But we do make some really great running shoes. This is not a criticism. This is a selective observation.

Imagine African Americans developing products for one of the most profitable industries in the world: Arms. We need to be in the business of manufacturing, advertising, distributing, and financing arms, and not just as consumers and victims.

Firearms Training

There are no firearm education and practice facilities (rifle or pistol ranges) located in or near our communities. That means access to formal firearm ownership and responsibility training for African Americans is mostly limited to those individuals who join military organizations or law enforcement agencies. This includes high school ROTC programs and private and public military academies. Shouldn't we have firearm training facilities in every neighborhood in every village, town, and city in America? The focus should be on firearms safety, civil responsibility, marksmanship, recreational competition and civic responsibility. Using military surplus small arms training simulators, our communities could learn responsible use of these tools. If local governments can get armored vehicles, robots, bombs and automatic weapons for local police departments, getting simulators for public education and safety should be easy.

I do not advocate that unconscious untrained individuals possess or operate any dangerous item or machine. Wherever there are police there's a firearms practice and education facility. Citizens should demand access to these facilities for practice, safety training, and to help build a trusting relationship between the law enforcement officers that we employ for public safety. When people are allowed access to education the whole world benefits!

Food for thought

No one is doing to an armed individual, what both the criminals and the police are doing to unarmed law abiding citizens all over the US. Educating citizens in firearm safety won't change any behavior for legitimate law enforcement personnel or people planning to do you harm. The prohibition of armed self-protection has turned otherwise law-abiding citizens into a commodity for America's private prison system and an inexhaustible source of revenue for police. This war on guns just like the war on drugs has turned our communities into the killing fields reminiscent of the war on alcohol. Only now the innocent victims are not just the unwanted people but everyday working Americans and their children living in gun free zones. Doesn't that sound stupid, "Gun free" zone? Apparently, criminals and police can't read.

Most African Americans live in large urban areas where our basic human rights have been denied for so long that we now unconsciously surrender our rights based on manufactured fear. Most African Americans are law abiding people who wouldn't purposely circumvent the law to perpetrate crimes against their neighbors. Young people have always behaved with reckless disregard for others. All gun control laws are directed at law abiding citizens. The proliferation of laws is not crime prevention.

Law enforcement is a booming business with free advertisement provided by news and entertainment media organizations for political propaganda and psychological terror for profit. The more laws you have the more opportunities the government has to turn citizens into criminals. The more laws you make the less freedom you have. Access to common tools for self-defense shouldn't be restricted to law enforcement officers (on duty, off duty, suspended, retired, furloughed, or fired), government officials, privileged individual's, private security agencies, people living in rural communities, and people with criminal intent.

Government records demonstrate that people living in large urban areas are the most likely to be affected by common crime. Crime studies show that all crime is exacerbated in places where law abiding citizens are prohibited from exercising reasonable self-protection and the police exercise life and death autonomy over the people. This is especially true in socially declining communities.

New York, Boston, Philadelphia, Detroit, Chicago, Washington DC, Atlanta, Dallas, Oklahoma City, Seattle, Oakland and Los Angles. In cities like these where large numbers of African Americans, Latinos/Hispanic, naturalized citizens and new immigrants from all over the world live, knives, dogs, and firearms as a means of self-protection have been outlawed, severely restricted, or prohibited in the name of public safety. But no one feels safe.

All of the above-mentioned cities enacted and enforced excessive self-protection restrictions in the name of public safety, including prohibitions of dog ownership. The demonization of particular breeds caused property owners insurance cost to rise dramatically. Property owners were forced to leave their property unprotected because they employed the same breeds of dogs used by law enforcement, now labeled too dangerous for the public. When the dogs were gone the police, and the criminals preyed on and terrorized these communities until the economics of these areas collapsed. You can't keep what you can't protect!

Everyone knows

The descendants of Africans have been woven into the fabric of this country as permanent as any people ever to arrive here. Only our elected government officials and maybe some truly naive individuals can still pretend to believe that these social disparities are self-inflicted. Today we see a lot of movies about African Americans with inspirational messages about praying for freedom while other Americans are preying on us. There has also been a tsunami of news about government officials and law enforcement officers deliberately engaged in violations of existing law. Our representatives call those actions, mistakes rouge incidents by individuals when they get caught on camera. Every African American should know and understand that defenseless people can be enslaved. I'm not advocating that anyone take up arms to cause harm to another person or to incite

insurrection against any level of government or law enforcement.
I am advocating that any prohibition of self-protection with
common weapons is unconstitutional and should be ignored
for your own safety. Ask Robert F. Williams

No US citizen should have to request permission from the police
for a right that is guaranteed by the US Constitution. Every
American and now the entire world, knows that our government
officials have been complicit in every misinterpretation and
misapplication of the law regarding the rights of US citizens
of African ancestry. African Americans are still at the bottom
of the social economic ladder in the US. We're still vilified and
handicapped to rise to full citizenship or potential. Change
is going to happen whether you do anything or not. You can
choose to be either the master of change or the victim of it.

More about us

I am not advocating indiscriminately arming anyone. It is every
citizen's right to be armed. It is also every citizen's right not to be
armed if they choose. That is what makes us free. The right to
choose. Law enforcement officials and criminals should expect
everyone to be armed. Americans need to stop allowing an elite
group of people to deny us our full measure citizenship. I'm not
trying to cut anyone out of their share of extorting revenue and
resources from frightened people to fund our own subjugation.
Nothing will change even if you choose to be armed. Neighbors
who do not respect each other cannot be expected to trust each
other when confronted by a common problem. Remember the
right to be armed is not to be infringed upon by the government
at any level. Any state-imposed prohibition against Americans
right to self-protection should be abolished. Ask James Madison.

Challenge Three

As a result of complaints from some of our customers regarding the excessive noise coming from our Niggas and Bitches, Niggas Ltd. has developed a suppressor to resolve this issue. It will be called the Caucasian. The Caucasian is a silencer suppressor that is designed to eliminate the noise coming from Niggas and Bitches. There may be situations where loud Niggas and Bitches could disturb your neighbors, and some people just don't want to hear them. Caucasians will stop the noise and put your neighbors at ease. This 3-D printer developed suppressor is superiorly designed with an adaptive threaded end to quickly screw your Nigga or Bitch into a muffled whisper! Caucasians will not be cheap to purchase, but when it comes to keeping your Nigga or Bitch quiet nothing compares to a Caucasian. Simply put the Caucasian in front of any Nigga or Bitch and experience peace and quiet that only a Caucasian suppressor can deliver. If the suppressor gets stuck, it can be removed with a twist. Our Caucasian silencer suppressors will stop all unwelcome sound coming from your Nigga or Bitch, or your purchase price will be refunded. We have Caucasian silencers to suppress all Niggas and Bitches.

Time to try something different

For every miracle in the holy books of the world's religions, people had to do their part. Paint blood over the door, blow the horn, or kiss the betrayed, God helps those who help themselves. If you don't like the direction we're going, you can do something different. Choose a different path. If you're following a leader, they are going to lead you somewhere. If someone provides you with alternative directions, you can choose which way you want to go. We, African Americans need options.

We graduate from the best universities in the world. Universities our country's founders created. The same universities our ancestors were denied access to, and the seeds of separatism, discrimination, racism, and elitism are cultivated. And since the Emancipation Proclamation, African Americans manufacture less than all other people in the US. We own less property and experience more government restrictions than anyone else. We must do something different.

Who are we? Contrary to popular belief, we are not a collective cohesive unified clearly identifiable entity of citizens. We are however most likely to encounter disparate treatment in every aspect of US citizenry. Some would say, if you don't like it, leave. I can only reply that we're not going anywhere, and everyone should be prepared for change. If your only source of news is the corporate media outlets and infotainment social media then you most likely believe that African Americans don't care about the environment, technology, or anything other than entertainment, politics and crime. Do you really believe that all African Americans want more restrictive personal freedom for their safety?

On our southern border citizens are arming themselves against people entering this country to work for them. While in the cities where most African Americans live more restrictive gun control is being imposed on defenseless people caught up in the war on our streets. Our government is capable of attacking its own citizens in the name of public safety. Think about that the next time you vote for someone who tells you they intend to restrict constitutional rights. For the general good of the nation without provocation our government rounded up and interned thousands of innocent Americans of Japanese descent and forced them into concentration camps for our safety and theirs. While African Americans living in fear at home, stood in line to fight anyone for American ideals. Our unarmed disenfranchised predecessors were helplessly paralyzed to aid another clearly identified community of US citizens maintain their freedom. We had little idea what was happening to these people beyond what we knew could happen to us again if we resisted or interfered. We knew what being treated like non-citizen, and sub-human felt like because we were as defenseless as they were to stop it from happening. Is there any wonder why many Asian Americans feel little solidarity with us? I wonder what the US would be like today if Asian, African, Latino and Native Americans had organized demonstrations against the atrocity perpetrated on their law-abiding neighbors. Reparations are due for Japanese Americans. People who can resist oppression will resist when fighting for the right to exist. Ask the Palestinian people.

African Americans have been under siege since before we were recognized as some measure of citizen. We are surrounded and constantly under attack, for whatever anyone can take from us, including our lives. We're continuously bombarded with images of the government involved carnage in our communities, while we're being coerced to abdicate our common sense and basic means to resist the perpetrators of exploitation, extortion, and extermination.

Arms dealing, including research and development, manufacturing, distribution, sales, and theft has been lucrative for everyone except African Americans. We have been treated like Hebrews in Egypt, Jews in Germany, and women in Afghanistan, denied the right to self-determination. Why would we surrender this right to the government without cause or question? Maybe it's true that African Americans can't read or comprehend (public schools).

Going back to what we were before the 13th Amendment is not an option. The principles of America are not intended to favor the desires of the affluent to be more important than anyone else. Even a fish will fight for its life when caught on the hook of someone who intends to consume it. There are people on this planet who are willing to kill every living thing to control other people. Imagine African Americans collectively declaring that we refuse to recognize any government restrictions against possession of common weapons for personal protection in accordance with the constitution. That would mean keeping and bearing the same weapons as police officers. Dr. Martin Luther King Jr. advocated filling up the jails with civil disobedience against laws that don't protect your wellbeing. Others will tell you that would not be a good idea because African Americans are seen as suspicious and dangerous in popular culture. The government via the police is free to use deadly force against you for your protection. When you stop following rules that don't benefit you, there will be resistance and human evolution is always challenging. Ask Mahatma Gandhi.

Do you feel safe?

African Americans are mentally, physically, and economically paralyzed by law and a culture of tolerance! This has been our condition since arriving here. Is it the victim's fault? We are the children of centuries of abuse, torcher, and murder of colored people in America. Can we acknowledge that we suffer from traumatic stress at the genetic level and that directly affects everything about us? Go to any city in the US and visit the most middle class African American neighborhood you can find. Ask yourself if you feel safe there. And if you don't feel safe, imagine how the people who live there feel. We're afraid at home, afraid in your neighborhood, afraid, downtown and in the woods. We're afraid of the government, police, corporations, the media, our employers, our employees, our neighbors, you, your children and ours. America has never been a safe place for us or anyone else.

If you force rats into a corner they'll fight back and try to escape. If you force sheep into a corner, get ready for wool sweaters and lamp chops. Force African Americans into a corner and the media would have you believing that most of us will stay right there waiting to be used anyway you chose. Some of us will even pretend that they always wanted to be in the corner. We avoid rural communities because our children are subject to constant unwanted attention. We cling to cities where our children are denied parents because there are no jobs in the neighborhood, and everyone is presumed a criminal suspect and under constant threat of attack. We are surrounded 24 hours a day by a uniformed army and terrorist insurgents fighting for territory. And we the people are prohibited from protecting ourselves.

Next

I believe that African Americans are allowing the wrong questions to be asked regarding gun control. We don't manufacture or sell any guns legally in the United States of America. Most of us live in places where personal protection is prohibited and crimes against helpless individuals are out of the control of law enforcement agencies.

It's been more than fifty years since the March on Washington for Civil Rights. America even elected a president who embodied the melting pot ideal of America. So, why is the media still pretending they don't know that only the wealthy are doing better, no matter what your race, ethnicity, age, sexual identity, political party, or national origin, and that the police do a good job of protecting the affluent and themselves on the street and in the courts. You need to understand that if everything was equal, we wouldn't be talking about this. We do not manufacture any weapons in the US. They could simply stop selling guns and ammunition to us. Don't confuse jobs with ownership. Poverty and crime will continue to escalate until we can provide for our own welfare and prosperity. Ask Fred Hampton

Individual Responsibility

In the ongoing gun control and law enforcement debate we have lost sight of the concept of personal responsibility. Human beings have always been armed with some kind of tool for self-defense. Let's not be confused, no single person armed with a handgun or rifle is any match for gangs, police, or the military. But civil society can dissolve into chaos during a storm, a pandemic or a protest. Firearms are tools designed to give you a fighting chance for survival in the deadly land of the free.

I'm speaking to all African Americans. Not knowing what the right is before surrendering the right out of fear keeps us in a cycle of government and criminal abuse. Have we gotten so used to abuse that we blame ourselves and agree to more abuse? Crime will continue to escalate in our communities because we're willing to trust strangers who don't know or trust us, to protect us and our children. We have allowed ourselves and our children to be labelled armed and dangerous even when we are bleeding out in handcuffs. Why would you surrender your right to self-preservation to those who have blatantly abused us? African Americans need not have amnesia about our experiences as a clearly identifiable classification of people to the government, the courts, law enforcement agencies (especially local police), each other and everyone else. Even after the 14th Amendment, laws continue to be made to deny us rights of every measure, from the right to bear witness, to the right to privacy, to the right to live as you choose. The 2nd Amendment is a right that every single African Americans should fight vigorously to define, understand, maintain, enforce and exercised. Our children should be able to recite it like the pledge of allegiance. Don't confuse acts of crime with exercising your right to life, liberty, and happiness. Today, all African Americans might consider being armed as a form of peaceful civil disobedience. We should conduct ourselves with civility when we encounter criminals and law enforcement officers for our own safety.

Whether it is the federal, state, or local government, Americans are supposed to resist oppression of any kind. I wish I could say that using lethal weapons against each other with the primary intent of causing harm to another human being or animal is a modern phenomenon but it's not. There are countless ancient stories about individuals with weapons attacking and killing unarmed individuals throughout history. Stories of tyrannical governments using armed law enforcement units to attack, extort, and exterminate unarmed citizens in their own country. There are other stories of armed citizens staving off the armies of unjust governments. And stories of nations ensuring every citizen was armed and trained to use tools of self-defense.

Challenge Four

Niggas Ltd. is now introducing two custom holsters for our Niggas and Bitches. They will be called the Latino and the Asian. Both holsters will be state of the art, custom molded leather or composite materials to keep your Nigga or Bitch in its place. Whether you carry your Nigga or Bitch out in the open or concealed out of sight, our Latinos and Asians will keep your Nigga under control and easy to get to. The Latino will be made from the finest Corinthian leather from free range organically feed single source bovine cultivators and hand molded by skilled craftsmen to our exacting old-world standards. The Asian will be made from high tech composite fiber infused materials, AI designed, and 3D printed for perfect balance of acceptance and control, totally recyclable.

The Latino will be cheaper to purchase than the Asian, but when it comes to keeping your Nigga or Bitch in its place while being budget conscience the Latino is for you. But when you need the very smartest hardest working holster to keep your Nigga in its place and money is no object, you can't do better than the Asian. The Asian can also be molded to accept the Caucasian suppressor for your Niggas. Our Latino and Asian holsters will keep your Nigga or Bitch in its place and under control or your money back.

Why should you be armed?

I understand why many Americans can't fathom a reason for anyone other than soldiers and police to carry firearms. I also understand that many Americans can't fathom a reason for interracial relationships, same sex marriage, or abortion. These are interpersonal activities that may be perceived by some citizens as dangerous threats to our social order and should be made illegal to keep you safe. And just like the restrictions on civilian gun ownership these citizens believe that restricting these activities doesn't infringe on your right to live free from the fear of others. If guns are the problem, the police shouldn't have them? Maybe they should only be equipped with bibles to pray for peaceful encounters with Americans. But as someone said, you don't take a bible to a gunfight unless there is a gun hiding between the pages. Today is the most violent and corrupt time in US history. Since September 11th 2001 more people have been killed on the streets of our cities than the American military casualties of the Persian Gulf and Afghanistan wars combined. The Iraqi and Afghan people suffered casualties in apocalyptic numbers, citizens, loved ones, children, mothers, fathers, and friends. Their defenses were no competition for the weapons brought against them to cure an issue that can't be cured by force. If you cannot defend yourself, you will be abused. Ask the Nazis.

During the first quarter of the 21st century more government officials, law enforcement officers, business moguls, celebrities and church officials have been exposed for corruption, murder, robbery, kidnapping, human trafficking, gang membership, firearms violations and other illegal or inappropriate activities than in any other period in US history. These are the people demanding the public trust them with our safety. Remember we elect them while our freedom is being tricked away by a network of private and government entities that profit from our fear and our inability to provide for ourselves.

According to the news untold numbers of armed gangs roam the streets of America, mowing down each other and innocent victims with powerful automatic weapons and the police are powerless to stop them. Throughout our history bloodthirsty murderers and shameless inveiglers have been morphed into folk heroes with monuments and documentaries to celebrate their reigns of terror over the American people, and the weapons they used to frighten us. Criminals and the police profit and benefit from prohibition of anything you desire (sex, alcohol, drugs, guns) for your personal use. Ask California State Representative Leland Yee. The targeted murders on the street and collateral deaths are the result of police and criminals jockeying for control of territory and profits for both parties. These periods of terror subside when the prohibitions are ended, but law enforcement agencies always manage to gain new and more intrusive powers to control law abiding citizens.

After WWI, most US cities established laws that required citizens to request a permit to carry a gun open or concealed in public. Rarely are permits issued to African Americans. Today with all the police surveillance and new more restrictive firearm laws being enacted daily, crimes against law abiding citizens are soaring out of the control of government sponsored law enforcement agencies and escalating. Not that the police have ever had any control over anyone willfully disobeying the law. If the government and the police are incapable of protecting you, isn't it reasonable that you should protect yourself? Oh, I forgot again, "Public Safety"!

The laws against citizens being armed have been proven ineffective in preventing people intent on breaking the law from committing any crime. Most prohibitions in the US are ineffective in curbing or preventing illegal acts perpetrated by individuals determined to circumvent the law for something the people are willing to pay for. No law can or will protect you or your loved ones from the actions of mentally ill people or willful individuals.

When you're looking at the wrong end of an elephant don't be surprised when you get dumped on. The police should expect every US citizen to be armed and cooperative. If you are not a US citizen, you should not be armed in this country. Any prohibitions should only apply to non-citizens. As citizens we should reconsider allowing elected officials and celebrities to redefine the basic rights of Americans in the name of "Public Safety". This idea of state controlled public safety is a lie used to curtail the freedom of citizens. The privileged people can afford armed security and bodyguards for personal protection. People who cannot defend themselves are subject to abuse, robbery, and murder.

A scary thing

Yes, a gun is a scary thing to have lying around your house where a child could have access to it! So is the car in your driveway. I know it's not a fair comparison because driving is a privilege, and you wouldn't leave your car keys where disobedient children can have access to these dangerous tools. And most cars are not specifically designed as weapons. But the knives in your kitchen are deadly weapons and you teach your children proper handling, care, and responsibility for these tools. Still every now and then you slice a finger. Accidents happen. Isn't it equally scary to be afraid to walk in your neighborhood day or night for fear that you will be accosted by people meaning you harm, and you have no ability to defend yourself? Or that your home will be invaded by criminals or police whether you're at home or away? Or that any police officer can accost you like a criminal just because of the color of your skin and the neighborhood you happen to be in? I agree, Americans shouldn't have to carry any weapon to protect themselves from other Americans. But you know what happens to people who cannot protect themselves. Ask women around the world, from the victims of domestic violence to victims of mass genocide.

We've all seen images of defenseless people around the world abused by gangs, terrorists, police, and government armies. Images of atrocities from Germany, Bosnia, and Nigeria stir our emotions to the point of wanting to arm these victims of terror to give them a fighting chance. But when the media presents images of the carnage on the streets of America, they resemble episodes from some television crime drama with the police assuring us that everything is under control. As the economy deteriorates further for the masses of unemployable people living in our cities, homelessness and crime will increase and they will be systematically directed into lower-income working-class communities. History reminds us that people without means to provide for themselves will turn to their government for assistance or to crime for survival, and against each other to get what they need. This is not an argument for whether guns are dangerous. Cars are dangerous, killing more people every year than all the gun related deaths combined. But it's not a fair comparison because driving is a privilege. Dead is dead, but if you compare tool to tool, even if you compare by numbers owned, guns and their owners are safer than cars, drivers, and passengers. To keep and bear arms is your right according to the constitution. No firearm has ever been convicted of murder. Food for thought! So now ask yourself:

Handguns

Most firearms related deaths in the US are not drive-by shootings, mass shootings in schools or theaters, or attacks on police officers as the mass media, social media, law enforcement agencies, celebrities and government officials would have you believe. Suicide is the leading cause of gun related deaths. Most crimes don't involve the use of any firearms at all. Those that may, like armed robbery, battery, and murder, a handgun is the weapon of choice for both the criminal and the police. Battery, rape, robbery and stabbings are perpetrated intimately close with the victims. Rarely are long guns (rifles and shotguns) used by perpetrators for this type of crime on the street. No law or law enforcement agency or well-meaning politician can protect you from this kind of encounter. Handguns are designed for personal defense during up close and personal attacks. Our military issues handguns to war fighters as a weapon of last resort for self-defense. Today's handguns are specifically designed for use within a zero to fifteen feet range. Most rapes, robberies, and murders of individual law-abiding citizens are perpetrated in this range. People that intend to do you harm will walk right up to you and take what they want. Money, cell phones, computers, your body or your life because the law prevents you from using the same tools every criminal and law enforcement officer uses for their own protection.

Criminal perpetrators believe that you are venerable to be accosted at close range because of state and local laws that restrict every means of self-protection (dogs, knives, and guns) for law abiding citizens. In most instances of up close and personal crime, the perpetrator is more than willing to take the risk that the victim will not fight back because of these prohibitions. No criminal will accost you from across the street. They can't steal your cell phone during a drive-by. You can be issued a traffic ticket though the mail, but criminals must enter your personal space to batter, rape, or rob you. A handgun is the best defense against any person, animal or vehicle forcing its way into your personal comfort zone. That zero to fifteen feet range is where a handgun could deter a perpetrator and save your life. Just remember comparing handguns to modern military machine guns is the firearm equivalent of the abacus to the computer.

People walk up to us every day on the street, up to our vehicles, our homes, our loved ones, asking for money and a multitude of other reasons unknown to victims. Law enforcement officials and criminals approach us with intentional purpose because they believe that we are defenseless and frightened. We are expected to obey both police and criminals without challenge because of laws that clearly violate our natural right to self-defense. Law abiding citizens willingly cooperate with the police in recognition of our civic duty and out of fear that we will be profiled as potential criminals because of where we live or the color of our skin. These encounters are becoming increasingly deadly for defenseless people.

The government, through the proliferation of laws, continues to employ the proven ineffective method of prohibition as crime prevention. For more than a century gun control has had a phenomenal negative effect on public and individual safety and the economy. Prohibition as a method of crime prevention has never prevented any criminal act from happening to any victim. But these laws have made many attorneys, judges, congress members, prison operators, police departments, undertakers, and others connected to the crime and law enforcement industries very, very wealthy. These laws have also given law enforcement agencies the totalitarian powers of fascist dictators over US citizens. Obey their command or die. Gun control sounds good to frightened people who don't understand that these laws turn law abiding citizens into criminals for merely possessing a tool commonly employed by police and criminals for their self-defense. Prohibiting personal protection doesn't protect anyone but criminals and police. The federal government is responsible for providing our national defense. That includes all the states and territories, enlisting our children as volunteers and by conscription to defend against all enemies of the constitution. The police are employed to assist the public during emergencies, assist the public with maintaining civil order, and to assist the public with bringing criminal suspects before the court for justice. The courts are responsible for upholding and enforcing the law. The congress is responsible for making laws and changing them when citizens or national concerns demand a change. None of these institutions are responsible for your individual safety, defense, or protection. That's your responsibility. Ask any insurance company.

No police officer or other privileged person would consider going anywhere without personal protection. Don't be confused, your personal firearm will not protect you against any organized groups, gangs, well-trained police officers or the military. But firearms are very effective for defending yourself and your family against individual perpetrators you may encounter. Firearms give you a fighting chance, an equalizing force and the element of surprise against being accosted, attacked, or killed on the street or on the trail. There are countless millions of incidences of armed individuals deterring crime by the use of firearms that go unreported because the police cannot report on incidents that they cannot or will not verify. And the police may confiscate your weapon because brandishing is illegal even if this simple act saves your life.

CCW letter to Congressional Black Caucus members

Dear Caucus Members,

California concealed carry weapons law requires military veterans to request and receive their constitutional rights from state and local law enforcement agencies. In the State of California, non-compliance with the CCW will result in mandatory confiscation of property, prosecution, fines, and imprisonment. This seems fundamentally wrong. I'm not a lawyer, but these laws seem to violate federal laws. This law essentially renders veterans to be disarmed "Prisoners of War" declared by the state in which we reside in or travel through. These laws criminalize all veterans, but especially, Black veterans because of our physical and cosmetic features which may be perceived as a risk to public safety. Veterans, like all law-abiding citizens, expect equal protection against unconstitutional and discriminatory laws nationwide. These laws severely restrict the rights and liberties of veterans by criminalizing weapons possession when no crime is being committed. It requires veterans to request our rights from state and local law enforcement agencies as if we were members of a conquered enemy army. For veterans' simple possession of a firearm should never be a crime anywhere in United States of America.

US military service members, veterans, give a solemn sacred oath to protect and defend the Constitution of the United States of America. We give this oath freely, without hesitation, reservation, or purpose of evasion. That oath did not end with an honorable discharge from active national defense service. Background investigation on military service members is more intensive, invasive, and thorough than those performed for most law enforcement officers, and many of us have held our nation's highest security clearance classifications. Even after discharge, veterans may be compelled into service when service is required. How then can veterans be required to request any of our rights from any state or local law enforcement agency?

Veterans are not adversaries or enemies of law enforcement. We are indispensable partners of law enforcement in maintaining order, deterring crime, and building safe civilized communities. Armed law-abiding citizens, especially veterans, are a crime prevention force multiplier for their communities, government, and law enforcement during tumultuous times and national crisis. Who's watching your home when the police are focused on big event crime and distracted from watching over you tonight? Veterans are the intricate unremovable thread woven into the fabric of our nation that holds it together and keeps us free. Criminalization and incarceration of veterans for simple possession of a firearm can't be an acceptable solution to America's crime and policing problems.

These laws have little to do with public safety or anyone's chances of becoming a victim. Everywhere you look there are armed individuals on our streets with weapons in clear view. And we, the public trust that those individuals do not pose a threat to our safety even when there is a mountain of documented evidence to the contrary. Police and privately contracted security agents have been proven to be as capable of misusing firearms as those individuals with clear criminal intent. I live in a state where veterans are being treated as criminally unfit and unqualified to possess and operate the same basic tools issued to us for defense of the nation. These are the same tools used by law enforcement agencies and private security organizations. These laws portend that veterans can't possess a weapon without having criminal intent or becoming some other risk to public safety because of the weapons influence over their actions. Every encounter you have with a law enforcement officer is an armed encounter. We can only pray that these encounters are lawful and civil.

These concealed carry laws restrict the liberty of law-abiding Americans based on the acts of individuals with clear criminal intent, mental challenges, and other issues that have nothing to do with individual liberties. Too many veterans' lives and liberties have been taken as a result of these laws and abusive ineffective methods of crime prevention such as accosting citizens for perceived suspicious behavior. This particular method of policing has been proven to be very effective at criminalizing veterans. Based on physical and cosmetic profiling, believed by a police officer to represent a risk to public safety, even without a report of crime, you can be detained, searched and interrogated on the street without arrest or articulation of a crime. Most African American veterans live in areas where public possession of a firearm is prohibited for all citizens except as permitted by state and county law enforcement agencies. Our basic human right of self-defense is severely restricted by these laws while violent crime is reported to be out of control by the police and the media. The criminal possession of firearms will continue to escalate as new laws are being created to criminalize Americans for behaving like intelligent responsible citizens. Greed, governance, and law enforcement practices may all be part of the problem along with community complacency and restriction. Militarizing the police and disarming citizens can't be the only answer to crime or policing. Criminal convictions of individual police officers and federal supervision of local law enforcement agencies nationwide should be enough evidence that Americans must take a different approach to public safety and law enforcement. Ask yourself what law gives police autonomy over citizens and what law protects police when they are accused of crime?

It seems that you are being asked the wrong questions regarding gun control and African Americans. Aren't you tired of the wild-wild west model of policing, you know where the law can't distinguish good-guys from bad-guys, the people are afraid of the sheriff, every sheriff declares himself the law, every judge issued their own brand of justice, and gangs are out of control? While the government and the wealthy rake in the protection money from frightened citizens in the form of taxes, fees, and fines for public safety. An American president once said if you've endeavored in a methodology for fifty years and it hasn't worked, it's time to try something else. The California law called the Mulford Act has been in effect since 1968. This law is just another "Black Code" law. This law has not prevented any individuals with criminal intent from being armed or committing crime and is not applied equitably or consistently statewide. These laws criminalize all veterans but especially Black veterans. Where most of us live you can be detained and searched by any individual police officer at any time, based on their alleged suspicion of criminal intent and your physical and cosmetic features. If you are found armed without their permission it will result in mandatory confiscation of property, prosecution, fines, and imprisonment. You may even be physically abused or killed during the arrest process as a consequence of officer 's training. California is so serious about this law, that police cannot be held responsible for your injury or death if you look like me and you're armed. It has cost the lives of too many unarmed and frightened citizens. Too many veterans are dispossessed of their property and freedom, imprisoned because of police preventing crime that has not been committed.

Maybe the Congressional Black Caucus can explain why government legislators vote ignorance over facts regarding weapons possession by veterans. Why would our elected representatives ignore the devastating criminalizing affect these laws have on veterans and all other law-abiding Americans? There must be at least one member of the CBC, former law enforcement or military veteran who can explain to the public how armed veterans are more dangerous to the public than suspended, furloughed, transferred, fired, retired, indicted or acquitted law enforcement officers and private security agents. Maybe they can explain why veterans should be required to receive permission to exercise any of our rights from state or local law enforcement agencies? The Congressional Black Caucus, along with the Department of Veterans Affairs, should vehemently oppose any and all CCW laws that place unnecessary restrictions and suspicion on our veterans who sacrifice their lives in selfless service to this country. The DVA collects and compiles data regarding health and safety issues affecting veterans and shares its findings with state governors nationwide. But the criminalization of veterans for simple weapons possession and the devastating effect of these laws on veterans, their families and communities have not been addressed by the DVA.

Any criminal will tell you that if you are already being treated like you're armed you may as well be armed. This is not a request for anyone arm to themselves. This is not a challenge to background checks, registration, license, safety and responsibility training. The requirement for veterans to have weapons possession identification could be resolved immediately. The Department of Defense could issue a Veterans Identification Card with reciprocal conceal carry privileges similar to law enforcement officers under the Police Protection Act. Our national heroes should not be subjected to the same level of distrust as common criminals for exercising a basic human and constitutional right. Honorably discharged veterans traveling throughout the United States are in immediate danger of losing life, liberty and happiness for simple possession of a weapon. These laws require urgent attention to be repealed. Americans are looking to you for leadership.

Respectfully, (add your name to this letter)

Rifles and Shotguns

Who needs a 30-round magazine on a military style weapon to hunt deer? No one! But if you're on private property safely operating firearms, who cares how many rounds the magazine holds. Any catastrophic event like earthquakes, wildfires, hurricanes, street demonstration, riots, terror attacks, floods, or pandemic can plunge civilization into chaos instantly. Modern rifles and shotguns are designed to be an effective deterrent to common threats at distance greater than 15 feet.

Limited capacity magazines for firearms could make sense if these rules apply to local law enforcement officers too. Patrol officers, detectives, and special operations officers should be limited to the same magazine capacities as the public. There is no reason that a police officer should need more than a six-round capacity handgun to perform their assigned responsibilities. Question: Why do the police need military grade automatic weapons and armored vehicles?

No law will prevent people from willfully breaking the law. No law will stop the crazies from doing crazy things. But shouldn't the local police also be subjected to the same laws and restrictions as the rest of us? After all, how many shots does it take to issue a traffic citation or respond to a call for emergency assistance?

Now in California you're required to register rifles and shotguns as if they are not already accounted for by the manufacturer and distributor. I wonder where those records will be stored, on a cloud in cyberspace where hackers working for the any entity, government or private concerns can take the information and share it with everybody in a spirit of transparency.

It's hard to believe that so many law-abiding Americans are purchasing rifles and shotguns to commit crimes that the government needs us to pay for information they already have. Every legally manufactured and distributed firearm in America is already required to be accounted for by the manufacturer and the distributor. These records are required by federal and state firearm manufacturing laws. So why are states requiring additional traceability of these legal products? Could it be just revenue generation and criminalization of citizens for the perpetuation of the law enforcement industry?

AWB letter to the Congressional Black Caucus members

Dear Caucus Members,

The California assault weapons ban currently in effect caused the criminalization of military veterans for possessing some of the most common arms on earth. The California ban prohibits weapons with physical and cosmetic features the US government has been buying and issuing to our children since 1960. The features prohibited for weapons owned by veterans residing in or traveling through California include; pistol grips, thumb hole grips, adjustable/folding stocks, flash suppressor/muzzle brakes, sound suppressing silencers, vertical forward hand grips, detachable magazines, magazines with capacity greater than 7 rounds, magazine release devices/bullet buttons, barrel shrouds/rails, carrying handles and other features designed to provide the weapon and the user with optimum function ability, operational safety, improved control and accuracy, according to the Department of Defense. Non-compliance with this law will result in mandatory confiscation of property, prosecution, fines, and imprisonment. This law must be repealed.

The law is not about how the weapon functions or its legal uses. This is about how it looks. This is akin to vilifying and criminalizing some people for the way they look. This kind of thinking would lead to mass incarceration of citizens with certain physical or cosmetic features that could be associated with potential crimes not yet committed. Think of it this way, law enforcement officers look like military combatants but they're not. However, the potential for individual law enforcement officers to abuse their authority or weapons and become a risk to public safety is well documented. The real crime being committed in association with this law is the criminalization of physical and cosmetic features of a person or thing in order to confiscate property and incarcerate disobedient citizens. These laws criminalize all veterans but especially Black veterans for possession of common weapons. Black veterans know what it means to be profiled just because of your features. These laws restrict law abiding Americans because of the acts of individuals with criminal intent or mental challenges, misuse and accidents. This evidence cannot be confused with the legal possession and use of these tools by millions of active-duty military service members, honorably discharged military veterans, trained-law abiding citizens, and law enforcement officers nationwide.

California civilian state and local law enforcement officers are authorized for duty and personal protection, military grade assault weapons such as the M-4 (Armalite Rifle USA 1960) and the AK-47 (Automat Kalashnikov USSR 1950) type weapons. These weapons are assault weapons (automatic and select fire) restricted to military and law enforcement officers in the US. Semi-automatic (non-continuous, single fire) versions of these weapons are available to the public for lawful use nationwide. They look like modern military weapons but they're not. They can only fire one bullet each time the trigger is pulled. The term "Semi-automatic" means the weapon does not require manual charging (cocking and loading) after each shot fired like a manually operated firearm. But this weapons ban is not about how these weapons work or their lethality. The US has severely restricted civilian possession of fully automatic weapons since 1938.

California compliant featureless weapons like your grandfather's lever action hunting rifle (Winchester USA 1860) or war souvenir (SKS USSR 1945) semi-automatic carbine rifle are no less lethal than the civilian versions of the AR and AK style rifles California is banning. Both of the afore-mentioned featureless rifles are battle proven military weapons actually used in combat and are currently available to the public. With their beautiful wooden stocks and polished brass pieces they just look friendlier than modern firearms with state-of-art materials, enhanced ergonomics and improved safety features. Any weapon capable of killing a 200-pound human being at 300 yards is also capable of killing a 200-pound animal at 300 yards for dinner. The bullet size and power are restricted, and background checks are required to purchase ammunition in California. Entertainers, corporate journalist, law enforcement, and even some elected officials want you to believe that some bullets are less lethal than others and that you are somehow less dead if killed by a law enforcement officer.

The rational for prohibiting the physical and cosmetic features of these weapons is not based on truth, facts, science, logic, or public safety. No justifiable or objective evidence has ever been provided to the public by the California Department of Public Safety, California Department of Justice, California Department of Veterans Affairs or the US Department of Defense, explaining how any of the prohibited features create an operational condition so unsafe for the user that these features must be prohibited from the public and the weapons confiscated for public safety. The California prohibition makes the physical and cosmetic features of modern firearms a manufactures known defects, and the public should be entitled to actual and punitive compensation for deceptive business practices that risk individual, public safety, and the safety of our people in uniform.

California legislators have chosen to ignore the scientific data collected during ten years of federal government prohibition and independent studies (1994-2004) of assault style weapons. The study concluded that these features have no compelling effect on crime or danger to public safety. The federal ban was repealed in 2004. In 2005 the US Supreme Court ruled that police have no constitutional duty to protect the public. The People of California have the California National Guard and the US Military to address any act of terrorism or incidences of insurrection inside California or the United States. The police are neither military nor militia. They're supposed to be "Peace Officers" employed to assist the government in maintaining order, assist the public during emergencies, and to assist the People with bringing the accused before the courts for justice.

California has spent billions on a lie that will cost taxpayers billions more by criminalizing, disarming and incarcerating veterans who pledged their lives to this country. If modern firearms are too dangerous for active service members, veterans, and trained law-abiding citizens to possess and use for lawful purposes, they have to be too dangerous for police. Blaming the tool for the act of the carpenter is not a reasonable explanation for the ban. California law enforcement agencies continue to acquire military versions of these weapons containing all of the prohibited features for their personal use, safety and defense. These laws criminalize all veterans but especially Black veterans for having physical and cosmetic features which may be seen by some as a threat to public safety. Veterans, like all law-abiding citizens, expect equal judicial protection against unconstitutional and discriminatory laws nationwide. These laws severely restrict the rights and liberties of veterans when no crime is being committed.

I can't imagine that the majority of veterans could be considered criminally unfit and unqualified to possess and operate the same tools as law enforcement officers without some criminal intent.

I do not believe that the people of California can allow the police to have weapons with physical and cosmetic features determined to be too unsafe and too dangerous for veterans. This means that whatever weapons or features of weapons "We the People" can't have, the police (law enforcement agencies at the state and local levels) should not be allowed to have as a matter of public safety. Including body armor, military weapons, electronic weapons (Tasers/stun guns), chemical weapons (pepper spray/mace/tear gas), and explosive weapons (bombs/grenades).

Where I live crime against the public is out of control. Greed, governance, and law enforcement practices may be part of the problem along with community complicity and media focus. Criminal convictions of individual police officers and federal supervision of local law enforcement agencies nationwide should be enough evidence that Americans must take a different approach to crime and public safety. Militarization of police and disarming law-abiding citizens has not been an effective answer to violent crime in America. Every encounter you have with a police officer is an armed encounter. We pray they these encounters are lawful and civil.

Veterans are not adversaries or enemies of law enforcement. We are indispensable partners of law enforcement in maintaining order, deterring crime, and building safe civilized communities. Armed citizens, especially our veterans, are a crime prevention force multiplier for our communities, the government, and law enforcement during tumultuous times and national crisis. Veterans are the intricate unremovable thread woven into the fabric of our nation that holds it together and keeps us free. Criminalization and incarceration of veterans can't be an acceptable solution to crime. These laws have little to do with public safety (your chances of becoming a victim) or the weapon's function (how many bullets it can fire at a time) or its legal uses (building, collecting, customizing, trading, competition, hunting, and defense). This is a criminalize and confiscate law disguised behind a manufactured public safety danger. Firearm ownership and training are strong family and community building activities.

America is a country of laws so complex and complicated that even the people who write them don't understand them. Maybe the Congressional Black Caucus can explain why California legislators would vote ignorance and propaganda over truth or facts about firearms. Ignoring the devastating criminal effect these laws have on veterans and all law-abiding citizens is not the answer. There must be at least one member of the CBC, former military or law enforcement veteran who can explain to the public how the prohibited physical and cosmetic features of modern firearms are a danger to civilian users but not to law enforcement users. Are the bullets fired from police weapons less lethal or less devastating to an individual hit by them? The Congressional Black Caucus, along with California Department of Veterans Affairs should vehemently oppose both the assault weapons ban and concealed carry laws based on the criminal condition in which they place veterans. The CDVA collects and compiles data regarding health and safety issues affecting veterans and shares its findings with the governor of California. These laws place unfounded unnecessary restrictions and suspicion on our veterans who sacrifice their lives in selfless service to this country.

But before you agree to imposing any more gun control measures on Americans, please consider the following: President John F. Kennedy, Bro. Min. Malcolm X, and Rev. Dr. Martin Luther King, Jr were all shot with California compliant featureless weapons. But they were murdered by the people who shot them. Today while many of our elected and appointed officials are diligently working to protect our immigrant population from harmful discriminatory legislation, the State of California is criminalizing veterans and confiscating their property based on lies. The US government is providing military versions of assault weapons to civilian freedom fighters around the world. There can't be a real ban on assault style weapons as long as police are allowed to have them according to the 2004 federal AWB findings.

Don't be confused, this is not about the police. They're just a clearly identifiable group whose features the public has preconceived assumptions about that may not be based on truth or facts. This is about the way something looks. Every night there is a broadcast crime drama just before the nightly news of crime somewhere in America. The government, police representatives, and the media are struggling with the image of law enforcement in America. In any given week the police are seen as saints and sinners, saving and killing children, enforcing and breaking the law in the same broadcast. But we can't imagine our society without them. If these weapons must be kept from the public, they must be banned from possession and use by state and local law enforcement as a matter of public safety.

At present neither California Department of Justice nor the US Supreme Court are hearing challenges to California's gun laws. This is not a challenge to or attack on law enforcement. This is a concern for public safety. Many of our elected representatives believe that law enforcement officers should be armed and trained like the military for our protection. These representatives must also believe that civilians should only be armed equivalent to subjects and slaves protected by their masters. What makes Americans unique among the people of the world is our individual right and responsibility to defend our laws, each other, and ourselves. For veterans' simple possession of a firearm should never be a crime. California criminalizes veterans for possession of common weapons when no crime is being committed and criminalizes weapons for common features. Please join veterans in demanding the President of the United States of America immediately address this assault on liberty based on how something looks. Honorably discharged veterans traveling throughout the United States are in immediate danger of losing life, liberty and happiness for possession of common weapons for lawful purpose. These laws require urgent attention to be repealed. Americans are looking to you for leadership.

Respectfully, (add your name to this letter)

Challenge Five

Niggas Ltd is proud to introduce its very own line of self-defense training aids for civilian and law enforcement education: The Woody.

A Woody is not a firearm, but it is designed to approximate the shape and ergonomic advantage of modern rifles and handguns for anyone seeking practical defense training where firearm practice facilities are not available, or they don't teach home-defense or urban survival to the public.

Civil disorder can explode into violence out on the street or inside your home without warning. Chaos doesn't happen from a fixed position at 25 yards. This is marksmanship training, available at most public shooting ranges. Marksmanship and firearm safety training are essential components of responsible firearm ownership. Equally important is learning how to identify potential threats on the streets. Understanding what objects and building structures can provide a defensible position for you. Learn how to protect your family and home without firing a shot. A Woody is not a firearm, you can train at home without the possibility of accidental discharge. A Woody is a tool that everyone can handle. Get in the habit of pulling your

Woody out to play with. Walk around the house with it in your hand. Think about what you could do with the real thing.

Every Woody is made of wood. Your Woody will be made to order from a variety of locally available wood species. Cheap to purchase, safe for everyone to handle, and you never have to get it loaded. It feels good in your hands. They have a natural point, and you can choose from a variety of popular handgun and rifle profiles.

Niggas Ltd guarantees that you will be glad that you wrapped your hands around our Woody. As a training tool nothing is safer. Woodies are easy to get and fun to play with no waiting period and no permission required. Take your Woody out and let everyone handle it. Make it a safe and practical group activity using these remarkable tools. Once they have your Woody in their hands, they'll want one of their own. We offer finished and unfinished Woodies to fit your preference, need, and budget. Choose a hand rubbed hardwood long assault style Woody or an unfinished multi-layered composite short Woody ready to be pulled out whenever you're in the mood to practice taking care of yourself.

Practicing armed self-defend at home or in public is a valuable skill when running is not an option. Remember to always be careful when handling your Woody in public because police can't tell the difference between your Woody and something really dangerous.

Gun Registration

Registering your weapons with any kind of government agency has only a very limited and deliberate purpose. That is for the government to know where the guns are when they come looking for them (notice that I didn't say, confiscate them). Does your state share or sell your vehicle registration information to private companies or organizations for data analysis? This is one of the issues why gun registration is an expensive public safety farce. Another issue with these laws is that guns can be illegally manufactured, transferred, stolen, lost and recycled into the hands of people who will never register them. Each legally manufactured firearm is required to have a unique serial number connecting the weapon to the manufacturer. That includes critical components such as the barrel of so-called ghost guns. When a manufacturer legally transfers a weapon to a distributor the unique serial number is tracked by both. Legally transferred weapons are tracked to the first retail buyer by the distributor. What happens to the weapon after that is out of government control. This should have resolved the registration issue for all legally manufactured firearms. So why are individual citizens paying states to register firearms that have already been registered by the manufacturer and distributor with the federal government? This is not an attempt to shift the blame from the perpetrator of illegal use of a firearm to the manufacturer. This is only a method of firearms registration and traceability that guarantees that all legally manufactured firearms are registered and eliminates the need for additional registration.

Background Checks

Let's have more intense background checks! But before you run out to vote for more intrusive personal information requests consider this: If the current FBI screening process for firearm ownership allows prohibited persons to purchase and register a firearm, how is that the fault of law-abiding citizens? Maybe the process has been outsourced due to labor cost in the US. If you drop your secrets in the ocean don't blame the ocean for taking them everywhere, including to people who intend to do you harm. How many government data breeches have there been? Who owns guns, how many, what types, and where they're kept is supposed to be a secret, especially from the government. Ask George Washington.

The Government knows best

The government of the United States of America has always been divided. We call this a two-party system. It is adversarial by nature. It allows balance for the benefit of all citizens. When the government is out of balance, the government starts to act like it knows what's best for the people and forces them to comply. This is what fascism looks like. The American people know how to reduce the crime in their communities, but the government keeps forcing more restrictions on us for our safety. If firearm safety is the issue, why aren't we teaching it in our public schools? Media sources report the Iranians are teaching it to their school children. If teaching driving safety in schools has resulted in a significant reduction in new driver accidents, isn't it reasonable that providing firearm education in our public schools could help reduce incidents and accidents?

A boy accidentally discharged a firearm found at home that allegedly was not secured in accordance with state law resulting in his sister's death. Instantly there's a renewed call from elected officials and law enforcement agencies to spend taxpayer's money on gun buy-back programs to address this issue. I wish they had the same passion for regulation every time a young person, new driver is involved in a fatal vehicle accident while texting or under the influence or being distracted relying on smart car technology to save them. Before we know it, the majority of vehicles on public roads will be autonomous and the access to manual driver input will be limited to law enforcement and the privileged. War can be fought with autonomous machines right now, but there will only be human casualties. I'm not suggesting suppressing the advancement of technology. All machines are designed to make life easier and safer for human beings. So, why aren't the costs of living, health care, and taxes going down? We have the highest number of mega-wealthy people on the planet. They are so privileged by wealth they can ship their vehicles and friends into space, while workers sleep on the street outside their places of employment. Maybe some smart person can explain how when technology displaces people, the cost-of-living increases for the people who have been displaced. It's like saying you're free now but you are not needed anywhere. Your contribution of labor, knowledge, skill, and blood to this society has been made unnecessary, safer, cheaper, and efficient by machines. Ask the Emancipated Americans.

During WWII, the German people say that they couldn't tell the difference between the police and the army. There were so many layers of secret government law enforcement the people couldn't trust family members for fear of arrest. The government commanded ultimate control over the people and their lives in the name of making them safe from each other. They did this in the open where everyone could see what happens when you don't comply with the authorities. The demonization of undesirable people didn't happen overnight. It had been going on since they arrived. Poverty was blamed on them, while the economy was booming for the wealthy. The increased control, being focused on the undesirable, resulted in mass incarceration of law-abiding citizens before the war began. By the time the world was outraged, people were being exterminated by the millions. The world had a hard time recognizing the problem because this was the model for dealing with unwanted people. Disarm, dehumanize and control them by any means necessary. This is how the US is beginning to look.

We cannot afford to blindly trust the government, the police, the corporations, the church, or each other. Armed people have nothing to fear from unarmed people. The police and the criminals have tried to convince us of this fact but we still refuse to believe it. We've spent billions on law enforcement and a criminal justice system that continues to treat African Americans as less than full citizens by denying us the right to self-defense in an active combat zone.

Our representatives (elected, appointed, and adopted) will legalize every illegal drug and every despicable act before they will agree that all Americans no matter where we live have the right to protect and defend ourselves, our family (biological or adopted), and our property without infringement by the government. It's easier to control distracted, intoxicated, defenseless and frightened individuals and groups.

African Americans believe in defending this country against all enemies. Corrupt government officials have openly admitted without an official declaration of war that a war against crime, drugs, and guns is being waged on our streets nationwide and we have been identified as the prime suspects and enemy of the people. Americans should be expected to assist each other for the safety of our communities and not waiting helplessly for the police to arrive. You be the first responder. You don't need the police to make your neighborhood safe for you.

The government has proven that it is not very good at protecting Americans from Americans. This is not about race, sexual orientation, religion beliefs, national origin, political affiliation or occupation. Take a look around the world. What made this country unique is the idea that all people are created equal with certain inalienable rights. Ask Abraham Lincoln. Honest Abe ordered the military to arm willing Negros and let them fight for their freedom.

But what the African American people have been getting is a smoke screen of fear by elites who only offer more control over law abiding citizens to address the issue of disparate treatment. Every firearms expert and industry leader has testified that no additional restriction on gun ownership or possession is going to affect anyone but law abiding victims of law. Crazies, criminals, willing individuals and law enforcement officers, intent on protecting themselves will ignore the law at our expense. The real problem is not with our representatives, the media, criminals or the police. The problem is with us, "We the People". We keep getting lost in the labyrinth of an illusion of safety and manufactured fear of each other. Can you think of a time when the government was not collecting information about everyone, and sharing that data with adversaries and allies regarding your habits? The government can't keep secrets and we the people are predictable. All the information/data about Americans that the government doesn't mishandle, it sells to anyone willing to pay for it.

Challenge Six

Niggas Ltd., creator of the Nigga and the Bitch is proud to announce the birth of the newest member of the Niggas Ltd. family, the Bastard. The Bastard is a single propose, pump action, 12-gauge shotgun designed specifically for personal protection and defense. When home invasion is a serious and constant threat, the Bastard is the perfect home companion for you. Constructed of stainless steel, carbon fiber, computer designed and totally, recyclable. The Bastard has the shortest barrel length allowed in all 50 states. It has a folding/removable rear stock and a pistol grip for maximum control in limited room situations. The Bastard can be hidden in the closet or under your bed where it can be easily accessed when time and surprise is essential to the survival of yourself, your family, or your property. The Bastard has no hunting or sporting applications. The Bastard is strictly a personal protection and defense companion similar to the shotguns commonly used by police departments everywhere.

Simply take the Bastard from its hiding place, pump a load into the chamber and you're ready to keep your family safe. Because it's a shotgun it poses less danger of having a stray round damaging your neighbor's property and the sound of a

Bastard going off will let your neighbors know that something bad is going on. Take the Bastard to bed with you. Who's going to know? Just the thought of turning a Bastard loose on an intruder will give you piece of mind or return it before use for a full refund of your purchase price. Remember no matter which Niggas Ltd., product you choose, the Nigga, the Bitch, and now the Bastard, are all designed to serve and protect you.

California

This year hundreds of new laws went into effect in California. Hundreds of new laws! Did we have a shortage of laws in California or is this what happens when lawyers dominate our government representation? There shouldn't be hundreds of new laws anywhere. The proliferation of laws only erodes liberties. How can anyone know which one of hundreds of new laws they may have violated? Every time the law is delineated it weakens the law and liberty.

When there's conflict in the application of law on all citizens that law may be unconstitutional. In California, people who live outside of the city and county where I live can receive a concealed carry weapon license issued by their local sheriff, valid statewide. They live in common law counties. The county sheriff where I live refuses to issue CCW's without an overwhelming justification approved by the sheriff. I live in a charter county. People with a CCW can carry weapons into where I live. But I can't carry a firearm in public at all because the sheriff of Alameda County can issue what rights I'm entitled to based, on the sheriff's opinion of my character and their assessment of my chance of becoming a victim of violent crime. The state agrees with this interpretation of the

US constitution. The police can carry whatever weapon they choose and kill people where I live because they feel unsafe or threatened, but I can't protect or defend myself here. Don't you think there's something wrong with this? Sometime when people are defending themselves, people get killed. Ask Travon Martin and Oscar Grant. Don't let anyone, especially the police, try to convince you that protecting and defending yourself is taking the law into your own hands. Bad people are going to do bad things. It is your responsibility to protect and defend yourself, your family, and your property in this country. Yes, people are dying as a result of being forced to wait for someone else to protect them. I don't want your grandmother to have to carry a weapon to feel safe outside of her home. That's her neighbor's responsibility. A safe community doesn't start with police. The government is more concerned with disarming law-abiding citizens than it is with keeping you safe from the escalating violent terrorism perpetrated by criminals where you live. How are more laws that turn victims into criminals going to be the answer to crime?

Where I live

Since the beginning of the 21st century the police have killed more Americans than known criminals. Don't confuse the criminals with the crazies or the willing. The Alameda County Sheriff's CCW policy requires an applicant to supply credible evidence that "there is a documented, presently existing, clear and present danger to life, or great bodily harm to the applicant and/or his or her spouse, domestic partner, or dependents;" that "the danger of harm is specific to the applicant, or his or her immediate family, and is not generally shared by other similarly situated members of the public;" that police can't adequately address the danger; that the danger can't reasonably be avoided some other way; and that granting a permit is "significantly likely to reduce the danger." This is the standard law abiding citizens are expected to meet while most homicides in the county remain unsolved.

Oakland, California has one of the highest crime rates in America according to corporate news media. The city has a population of almost a half million people and a police department of less than 800 uniformed officers with another 2500 or so other armed law enforcement officers in the surrounding area supplemented by an unknown number of federal and private security agencies at their disposal. According to local news sources there's an indeterminate and growing number of bloodthirsty criminals alleged to reside within the city limits and surrounding municipalities. Do the math. It's impossible for the police to protect anyone in Oakland except for themselves. The last part of the sheriff's CCW requirement seems to contradict the intention to restrict concealed carry and justify on-demand issuance. Maybe that's why some sheriffs sell this privilege as a quid pro quo.

The average police officer in Oakland patrols the city in very expensive high-performance vehicle equipped with computers, weapons, emergency aid kit, cameras and other electronic surveillance, and an assortment of other police equipment including fully automatic military issue weapons costing a lot of money. The average police officer that you and I may knowingly come in contact with has a uniform, badge, ballistic body armor, semi-automatic pistol, electronic stungun, chemical spray, a collapsible steel baton, an on-body radio, a cell phone, on-body camera, a ticket book and an equally outfitted partner. They need all of these things to safely issue you a civil citation. A judge in the U.S. 9ᵗʰ District Court of California said, law enforcement personnel shoulder a duty to ensure public safety and assume different responsibilities, risks, and rights. It is manifestly rational for peace officers to possess and use weapons more deadly than arms available to the public in order to maintain public safety.

The average criminal suspect, apprehended, convicted, or on parole in the city of Oakland rarely has firearms on their person. The majority of firearms seized by the Oakland police occur during the so called "Gun Buy Back" programs and property searches. The firearm left in your grandparents closet is not a weapon on the street, and most of these weapons are legally owned, and not associated with any known crime. These are supposed to be no questions asked programs. It's a peculiar name for the process of paying citizens to turn in unwanted weapons. The program's name portends that the police provided the weapons to the public in the first place. Most gun shops will also buy used firearms from the public, but they don't intimidate or guilt anyone into exchanging their unwanted property for less than its actual value. There are no gun shops in Oakland or Alameda County.

I wish the media's pictures of confiscated weapons included guns with the trigger guards cut out to remove the safety lock required for all legal firearm ownership in California. At any hardware store you can purchase a device that will grind through the trigger guard to remove the cable lock security device the state has imposed on all legal firearms owners under the guise of safety and security. Yes, a safety lock may prevent a six-year-old from accidentally discharging a loaded weapon. But it will not stop anyone determined to do something criminal from stealing and using a weapon secured by one of these devices. It will hamper law abiding citizens from defending their lives and property when time is critical. Imagine a police officer having to remove one of these devices while on patrol. It would slow them down to the point of endangering their lives. What good is a personal protection device if you do not have access to it when your life is in imminent danger?

The most common arrest in Oakland is for traffic violations. Then drug and sex trafficking, robbery, battery, sexual assault, burglary, vandalism, and homicide. With the exception of traffic violations, suspects are rarely held responsible. Revenue generated from traffic enforcement is calculated into state and local budgets.

Incarceration for marijuana possession became so excessive and expensive that the state had to relax its drug laws to reduce overcrowding in the mostly privately owned and operated correction facilities with new prisons under construction statewide. And I haven't even addressed police misconduct, abuse, harassment, corruption, profiling, and shooting of unarmed citizens for which they are rarely charged or convicted. With a severcly understaffed, inept, corrupt police force and an unknown number of bloodthirsty criminal suspects roaming our streets. The City of Oakland, the County of Alameda, and the State of California have imposed some of the most restrictive firearm laws in the United States against the law-abiding citizens of Oakland. Why? Public Safety!

If the City of Oakland was serious about decreasing violent crime it would do something different. Take the police out of their cars and end all undercover police activity. Put all of them in uniform with rifles, helmets, and body armor. That way they can really look like the occupying force they portend to be. Install traffic cameras for revenue collection. Allow law abiding citizens to carry open or concealed weapons for personal protection. Millions of our tax dollars have been wasted on doing the same thing over and over while expecting different results.

Put more police on the street? Isn't that's like saying put more foxes in the hen house and raise more chickens for them to eat? If our jails are already overcrowded, that crime prevention thing we're doing isn't working. The police are not obligated to protect you or to prevent any crime from happening to you. When you are being accosted, assaulted, robbed, raped, and murdered, remember that! Wouldn't it be good to be able to defend yourself or someone else when you believe lives are in danger just like any individual police officer? Don't be confused. You are not going out looking for deadly encounters. You are not seeking to enforce anything on anyone. You are not taking the law into your hands. You are taking your life in your own hands.

The most powerful and ruthless gang where I live is the police. We train them, arm them, pay them and surrender our citizenship to them in the name of public safety and civil obedience. Only to be abused by these gangs gone military high tech. The out-of-control conflicts between the police and the public is being exposed through social media and demonstrations in the street, then aired on broadcast TV for entertainment and commercial advertisement. Ask the OPD. Unfortunately, those same tools being used to catch police behaving badly are also catching us bending the rules of colorblind privilege while disrespecting others. Ask Karen. The people's complaint of police misconduct, murder, extortion, intimidation, and evidence tampering, is against the culture of law enforcement and not just the conduct of individual officers. The real change that should be demanded requires changing the laws that give police total authority over citizens and qualified immunity.

I don't care what is wrong with anyone when they are in the process of doing me harm. I don't care what kind of family or social situation they come from when they are in the process of doing me harm. I don't care what mental, chemical, economic, or criminal condition they're in when they are in the process of doing me harm. I challenge the City of Oakland, the County of Alameda, and the State of California on common sense gun laws that make common sense.

This is the wild, wild, west where common citizens are so busy being distracted by wizards and electronic illusion that we can't see the social order we're paying for. My interests are not global. My concerns are local (why does my street look like the surface of the moon) and resources here are not unlimited (there are people living on the streets just looking for a chance).

Our elected officials, military leaders, and law enforcement agencies just stated yesterday on worldwide corporate news that our entire military; active, in-active, discharged and retired veterans are mentally ill and incapable of being trusted with any personal weapons. The military is considering banning all personal weapons on our military bases as a response to domestic terror. Active-duty personnel should be allowed to carry their service weapons at all times. They're soldiers 24/7, 365 and being made victims every day at home. Prohibiting civilians from basic rights is violation, enough of the constitution, disarming our service members traveling outside the safety of our bases in hostile domestic territory is treasonous. Is there a deadly war on crime and terrorism inside the US or not? If there is, I don't want to be defenseless and I don't want our service members at the mercy of criminals, private security contractors or police. The (add your city) police department has been at war with crime ever since the police department was established. And throughout our history the police have been involved in the crime business. Crime pays! Today an American can be accosted by any police officer without any knowledge of any civil offence and be killed by that officer in self-defense and this authority is not a crime? To the police, your life has no value that you should be able to defend.

The founders of this country warned against disarming the people. They knew what it was like to be robbed every day by a financially insatiable, corrupt and oppressive government. To be high jacked by violent opportunists and swindled by the righteous. To be murdered by hostiles, while trying to hold on to their property and prosperity. We have magically amended our laws to make law enforcement officers immune from criminal prosecution while citizens are forced to become victims in the name of public safety.

Somewhere in all of these laws to enforce our individual safety, we have forgotten what it is to be an American. We the people don't surrender our rights to the government at any level, gangs, terrorists, or frightened individuals. Think of yourself as a law-abiding citizen being American.

When your country's adversaries see your leaders in constant disagreement and distracted, your country will be challenged. If you're in a war you can't keep acting like you're not involved. People have, and they watched helplessly while millions of their own neighbors were exterminated by the people who were supposed to protect them. It's happening right now around the world. The prohibition on self-defense is killing Americans!

History only repeats when you didn't learn anything and didn't choose to change. America has flaws in its foundation and our weaknesses are seen around the world. Beheadings, drone strikes, kneeling on someone's neck, the reason for violence, only matters to the perpetrators, not the opposite.

How can the American people trust our state national guard when they have allowed gang members, police officers, and private security agencies to infiltrate these organizations? This is no different than members of the Taliban infiltrating the Afghan army. Our military shares secrets, tactics, and weapons with every kind of civilian law enforcement agency and private security organizations and foreign governments for our safety. Do you feel safe?

Every time a police officer kills someone, the police and the politicians claim that the officer's life was in danger. Look at it this way. If you rolled up on two people walking down the middle of the street and you yelled out of the window of your car at them to get out of the street. Are they obligated to follow your instructions? And if they don't, could you get out of your vehicle and shoot them for their safety? In the eyes of the world, our propaganda has remained focused on foreign affairs for corporate profits while turning a blind eye on the domestic war being waged on America's streets. If America is not safe for our police, soldiers, wealthy, politicians the press or the poor, it can't be safe for you and me either?

A letter to the world

Dear Competitors, Adversaries, Enemies, Criminals, and Terrorist,

Our people have been disarmed for their safety. Our army is under the control of private contractors with government oversight. Our military leaders are selected incompetents, highly paid corporate representatives in training, who do what they're told and are distracted and festinated by technology. And according to the corporate media, our military personnel are mentally exhausted and mentally ill. Our veterans are drug addicted and mostly prohibited from having access to any weapons. Our cities are densely populated with unarmed civilians who are used to hiding and waiting for someone to protect them. They also know better than to disobey the police. Our law enforcement officials pander to the wealthy and are susceptible to corruption and illegal unethical persuasions of all kinds. Our elected officials are well paid mysitics and magicians educated in argument and confusion, convoluting our laws into traps to extort money and resources from our frightened citizens. Our corporate and social media outlets are masters of illusion and deception, and they make it seem so real. We have everyone under control.

Sincerely,
The New United States of America

Why should you trust the government to protect your individual interest or safety?

If we hold these truths to be self-evident, why do so many government representatives advocate for keeping law abiding citizens defenseless? American citizens are under siege while elected officials and law enforcement organizations demand more restrictions on the law abiding. The government should be in the business of protecting us from terror, not prohibiting us from protecting ourselves! We cannot trust the government, the police, the corporations, the church, or each other with our individual safety. We're shown this every day and still we refuse to believe it. We have spent billions on law enforcement personnel, equipment, and training, to support a criminal justice system which continues to treat us as an inexhaustible commodity without a measurable or sustainable reduction in crime anywhere. Our presidents, congressional representatives, justices, governors, and mayors are willing to enact new laws while the existing laws remain unenforced, unenforceable, unjust and unbelievable. The police are cowboys still living in the wild, wild, west, believing that they are the law, and that "We the People" must obey them under fear of death.

Our elected officials must have a financial agreement with the owners of America's private prisons to maintain a high incarceration rate. That translates into the United States incarcerating more of its citizens than any other modern civilized democratic country. Our law enforcement system perpetuates its own growth and control by turning citizens into criminals for violations of laws the people don't know exist, seizing citizens and property, for crimes not yet committed. Crime continues to escalate nationwide while law enforcement agencies demand and receive more power and money for a service that doesn't work. New laws continue to be written in a language so complicated that even our law makers can't understand, can't explain and can't agree on, for reasons that defy logic. But the intolerable behavior of the police and the criminals has only intensified against their common resource, law abiding citizens. African Americans should never again allow ourselves to be voluntary victims of other people's fear. We have defended this country against its enemies. Our elected officials at all levels of government have openly declared a war against citizens perceived to be capable of crime not yet committed. Without an official declaration of war that clearly identifies the combatants, enemies, allies or objectives, we have given the police war powers over citizens. Our elected officials have proven how easily they're persuaded by campaign contributions, lobbyist perks, and celebrity. The US has so many laws today that no one can tell you what the law is. Ask Donald Trump. Every liberal news outlet promotes more restrictive gun control, while extoling the benefits of more armed police protection from you for your safety. African Americans have firsthand experience with being protected by people with the power of life and death over you, while being prohibited from any means to protect yourself or resist.

I don't need to predict what twisted people could be thinking. There are enough private organizations and universities collecting, sharing, and selling every possible exploitable characteristic of human life already. But even with all of the data collected and analyzed by everyone, we couldn't predict that someone would buy enough fertilizer to blowup a big government building full of children or that someone would use flying machines to murder thousands of human beings whose only crime was being at work. We still don't have all the information.

Advocates for the voting rights of people released from incarceration are pleading with the government to abolish this state-by-state voting restriction. Our law prohibits taxing any citizen without representation. These are the kinds of legal tricks from state governments that we have tolerated for far too long. People are being raped, robbed, and murdered (virtually and actually) by criminals, police, and each other. And the only solution our government continues to offer is further restriction on everyone who obeyed the law. If you don't have your protection with you, that is the same as not having any? Ask Planned Parenthood.

Whenever the government wants more money for our security it raises the fear level through enforcement of the laws of collection. At the local level that could be interpreted as intimidation and extortion by law enforcement via civil code violation enforcement and forfeiture of property without conviction. You know that driving is a privilege regulated by the state. Those of you who don't choose to drive, don't escape these laws or the fines and fees associated with them either. Traffic violations are issued to pedestrians and bicyclists for a variety of public safety reasons. Think of the amount of money being collected from you to keep you safe. Someone must pay for those traffic safety signals that too many individuals choose to ignore. The US Constitution is supposed to be the common law nationwide. That law is augmented, supplemented, and delineated by corruptible flexible state laws, which institutionalize disparate policies regarding citizen's rights. Remember many of our elected officials and law enforcement officers continue to be convicted of crimes involving mistreatment of defenseless people nationwide.

Our elected officials, including the president are trying to convince the American people that more intrusive laws will somehow keep weapons out of the hands of people with criminal intent or mental challenges. Nothing could be further from the truth. There is no evidence whatsoever that restricting your right to protect and defend yourself has stopped any murder of citizens obeying these laws. And some of those advanced civilized countries the celebrities mention in their analogy for gun control, practiced genocide against their own unarmed civilian populations throughout their histories and even today. Some of them struggle with the idea of equality without losing ancestral superiority based on interpreted entitlement.

If firearms are such destructively evil tools, why do we allow the police to have them? Why can't the police just pray for a peaceful outcome to tense situations like they expect for you to do? I live in a country where Martin Luther King Jr. was considered a domestic terrorist because he peacefully opposed the mistreatment of Negro people. Still today many of our elected government officials believe that we don't know our place and that they need police to control us. There has never been a more vital time for the US government to train and equip every willing and able citizen in the proper use of firearms. The government and law enforcement organizations agree that our common enemy is already here on our streets. But they can't distinguish them from us. Can you?

Why trust the authorities?

Our elected representatives and law enforcement officials are constantly being investigated for accusations of corruption and participating in every kind of activity that our laws prohibit. Our elected officials, law enforcement agencies, and judicial officials have been convicted of every kind of crime imaginable.

Our elected officials regularly vote to arm people in other countries to fight the same problems we have at home. Think about it, our money is being used to supply assault weapons to people in other countries for their personal protection and to fight oppressive governments. Did we enter into some secret agreement to arm the world and disarm Americans? Some of these grand ideas to arm other people have come back to haunt us in body-bags filled with our children.

Data Collection

The President should issue an immediate order that all current and past employees of the Department of Defense, the unencumbered right to be armed as a result of what the government calls a cyber-terrorist attack on all DoD employee's personal data, including security clearances information and current addresses (not just finance information). Federal employees not only are your finances at risk, but also more importantly your life and the lives of your loved ones are also at risk to an enemy so terrifying they have boldly attacked unarmed citizens in public in the presence of law enforcement. Government officials have allowed our secrets to be shared with our competitors and adversaries. Government officials have told us that because they don't own the satellites and computers used to connect us through the Internet, they can't control what happens to information in cyberspace. Everything about each, and every one of us has been compromised while under government control. Now our adversaries know who owns guns and where they're located. They also know that our police and political representatives are easily corrupted by power and money. The government and the police cannot keep you safe, but they're very good at protecting themselves at the people's expense. Ask Edward Snowden. There's video surveillance everywhere watching spying on us and our undesirable neighbors, then sharing the observations for profit and entertainment. Law enforcement agencies continue to collaborate with politicians, the court, corporations, churches and criminals sharing and selling information about you.

Challenge Seven

Niggas Ltd. is proud to announce our new environmentally friendly ammunition for Bitches and Bastard. The new ammo will be called: The Shit. The Shit is a shotgun shell loaded with scientifically treated canine excrement with customizable genetic markers to make each load easy to trace by law enforcement agencies. When home invasion is a serious and constant threat where you live, the Shit can help law enforcement agencies discover the perpetrators and your property. The Shit cartridge is constructed of biodegradable paper and hemp plastic for the shell materials and can be used in any shotgun. The Shit is loaded with scientifically treated canine excrement with unique genetic markers, pellets of recycled toilet paper, and reclaimed copper shot.

When used against any perpetrator, the Shit will leave a very strong odor of canine excrement on their clothes, vehicle, or body. Persons wounded by the Shit will require medical attention for the infection caused by the scientifically treated excrement. The scent can be tracked by law enforcement canines even when it cannot be detected by humans! Anyone who has ever stepped in canine feces can attest to the lingering and easily recognizable aroma. The genetic markers will help law enforcement agencies link the perpetrators to specific incidences of contact with the Shit.

Anyone hit by Shit from a Bastard will be easy to locate and identified by the unique odor and genetic markers or your money back. Remember, no matter which Niggas Ltd., product you choose, Nigga, Bitch, Bastard, or Shit are all designed to serve you. Get the Shit today. Warning: Both the blast and the possible bacterial infection from this Shit can be lethal.

Why should you trust the NRA?

Pick up any gun magazine at any news stand, bookstore, or gun shop in the US and you'll get a clear picture of the demonization of black people in the press. In one magazine there were more than three hundred photographs, articles, and advertisements without one single image or word by or about black people as responsible safety conscious gun owners. If you do see black people in these publications, they'll be in a military or law enforcement role because some people believe that you can trust a Negro in uniform. But African Americans can't. That has not been our experience. At the same time each of these magazines had articles and images romanticizing criminals and the weapons they used to murder and terrorize Americans. See for yourself.

The NRA is complicit with this false perception of African Americans as criminals through its continued advertisement and articles in these publications. And for all of you Negro, NRA members believing it represents every American's right, you need to ask them why they continue to advertise in what appears to be racist publications. You may also want to ask the

NRA where your visible representation is in the decision-making positions of the organization. Yet we continue to invest millions of our dollars in this organization through membership and the purchase of these products. We need to wake up and get into the firearms manufacturing business for ourselves. None of this is to infer that the NRA does not continue to provide real firearm safety training, fighting to preserve 2A rights for everyone. Remember the most powerful gun law lobby in America is the FOP (Fraternal Order of Police), not the NRA.

Why should you trust religious leaders to address your interests and rights?

Remember the story of what happened to Jesus of Nazareth. Religious leaders have been proven to be equally as corrupt, criminal, and inept as law enforcement agencies and the government at curtailing criminal activities. In many cases religious leaders have been complicit in the fight to circumvent your civil and human rights related to self-preservation. They work with the privately owned prisons to have criminals released back into the communities they terrorized through the revolving door of the criminal justice system. They also work with police and criminals on the street sharing information regarding community organizations, while spreading insidious instigations about their religious rivals. These religious leaders portend that their organizations are helping to maintain domestic tranquility in order to maintain their tax-exempt status in accordance with that old, outdated Constitution. Using the same feeble public vigils and tragic event driven demonstrations, religious leaders line up like ambulance chasers in areas under siege by criminals and police as evidence of their concern for the community. All three of these entities, criminals, law enforcement, and the church, have a vested interest in the continued destabilization of communities. Few outspoken religious leaders in African American communities have ever served the people as military combatants or chaplains. Many of them were born again in correction facilities as inmates. Yet, they're advising us, law abiding citizens, and veterans, to surrender our natural right to self-defense in a war that we can't survive with pleas or prayers alone. Many of these same outspoken leaders in the clergy also employ armed security for their personal protection. But they hold onto that freedom of religion part, of our constitution. Talk about tax breaks for the wealthy! Ask Rev. Jerimiah Wright.

Media's Influence

On-air media, print media, motion pictures media, and electronic social media, is how most people learn US culture and law today. Prior to the twentieth century, people who could afford to travel (soldiers, politicians, merchants, and wealthy people), told America's story to the world. History taught in public schools is reinforced and brought to life through the media. We should have learned that our right to free speech and self-defense are the pillars that hold up our American constitutional republic. Ask John Adams

In movies depicting the expansion west, a common theme is every settler, traveler, citizen, and foreigner was expected to be armed. These brave pioneers encountered every kind of adversity imaginable. Man, and beast alike would learn to respect them because Americans had guns. When you move into a new neighborhood, and establish your presence in that community, not all of your neighbors will accept you. Some will even use violence against you to communicate their status in the community.

I love watching "Westerns". Any movies made about European/ American western expansion. I especially love the ones that depict life during and after the American civil war. Everyone was armed. Everyone was expected to be armed, except for the newly emancipated citizens. Everyone was responsible for their own safety, except for those newly emancipated citizens. If you were not armed when force was the correct response to injustice or danger you would be provided with a weapon and taught how to use it. There were bad people in good places and good people in bad places. Government officials, mayors, sheriffs and their deputies were susceptible to the influence of money and power. The US Marshal could count on the citizens to support law enforcement with their guns and lives. Marshals were more respected or feared than the local sheriff, because Marshals seemed more impartial and less influenced by local authorities and money. But a Marshal's power over the people was often abused, such as deputizing family, friends, and criminals in their pursuit of their self-determined justice. There were also private security agencies like Pinkerton and Wells Fargo, bounty hunters, and gang members turned gunslingers, turned law enforcement agents. From the east to the west, outlaws evolved into law enforcement that engaged in deadly battles for territory, public resources, and power over the people. Today, just like in those movies about the "Old West", sometimes you can't tell the good guys from the bad guys. Law enforcement agencies have a long history of abusing citizens. When the people could no longer tolerate corruption of elected officials and law enforcement, the people would run the sheriff and the mayor out of town along with the bad guys. Sometimes the good people had to rely on the bad people to protect them from corrupt law enforcement. When that happens, law enforcement agencies resort to military equipment (revolver pistols, lever action rifles, and machine guns 1860) to maintain control over the people. Just so you know. Most African Americans are prohibited by state and local laws from being armed in public.

From the movies, documentaries, and news programs, everyone should know that when you can't tell the good guys from the bad guys, you need to be able to protect and defend yourself. Every night on the news, African American communities are turned into Hollywood western movie towns, where the sheriff and the outlaws shoot it up with each other, destroying property, endangering lives, and wreaking havoc on the town. In the movies, towns succeed when citizens stand together to root out the problem themselves.

Western movies brilliantly document the alienations of African Americans before and after the civil war. These movies remind us that at that time in our history, most citizens, new immigrants, and the newly emancipated, believed the US constitution was the law of the whole country. In Western movies you're taught that sometimes the people have to take up arms against corruption and violence in their communities. It's not hard to make bad guys out of people who don't share your values or that you want to believe are not equal to you.

Western movies illustrate the need for self-defense down to the individual. Movies show what an extremely perilous experience it was for Negros traveling west across America after the civil war. They had to endure merciless natural elements, dangerous animals, limited resources, no government support, heavily armed hostile people and new immigrants who blamed the victims of slavery for their own tribulations. These perils still exist for us today.

Since the official end of the civil war, the emancipated and their descendants have been expected to continue to accept life here as less than full citizens. And when we don't, new laws are created to keep us in our place. At the end of the civil war, literacy wasn't an issue for us. Former slaves had skills that could be traded for whatever they needed, and most people regardless of race, could neither read nor write in standard, English. African American citizens understanding of anything was irrelevant in the eyes of the law enforcement.

Everywhere the newly emancipated attempted to migrate, they became the victims of abuse and murder at the hands of armed citizens. Crime and government sanctioned violations of the constitution continue to be common encounters for the descendants of the emancipated. Yes, the movies illustrate there were problems for Americans of every kind, but only African Americans had to be emancipated to be recognized as some level of citizen. Everyone else has been naturalized with the full protection of the constitution. Naturally!

In the old west people wore their weapons in the open just like the sheriff. Citizens carried the same firearms as the army, sheriffs and outlaws. Police identified anyone attempting to help the people free themselves from the oppressive protection of law enforcement as outlaws. Teaching the people how to protect themselves was considered a waste of time and dangerous for law enforcement officers. Outlaws worked with the people. Instead of taking their firearms and aiding the perpetrators of abuse, they taught them how to use these essential tools, much like our military does for other people around the world today to combat terrorism.

The westerns warned us against more laws and local law enforcement. The images of corrupt inept public officials and abusive law enforcement officers was so prevalent in early days of Hollywood, the industry was forced by law enforcement lobbyists into making movies and TV shows with heroic depictions of police. From criminal to comical to militarized first responders the media has shaped our perception of police and police behavior.

I watch westerns because they give me the impression that the US was truly a free country with opportunities for everyone except for the newly emancipated. Ever wonder why you don't see a lot of Negroes in old west movies? There must have been hordes of Negros escaping the south and moving west to live like free people, real Americans. But the absence of Negros in these movies reminds us just how hostile and deadly post-civil war America must have been for them.

Negroes were prohibited from being armed, voting, testifying against anyone but other Negroes, holding public office, living where they choose, marrying who they chose, equal access to stores, restaurants, bars, hotels, transportation, hospitals, using the same toilet and drinking water fountain as other Americans. Rules enforced by the police, elected officials, the court, and the state armies. Westerns remind us that US citizens expect the right to be armed for self-defense and understand that not everyone with a badge is a good guy.

Why are there so many recent movies looking back reminding us that we still don't know our place in America? How can we continue to see full length docudramas testifying to atrocities perpetrated against us by every kind of citizen and continue to believe that the civil war ever ended? We must decide what kind of America we want to live in. Westerns movies show us what a scam the law enforcement industry is today. I don't even want to pretend that I know anything about how complex it is to serve and protect citizens that you have been trained to distrust and control as a police officer, or how expensive the law enforcement service actually is, but something is not right.

There have been a lot of movies lately to remind everyone that African Americans were slaves, subservient, and dangerous beings not to be trusted. There have also been a lot of movies reminding us that white people and the police are righteous superheroes, super genius, and direct descendants of God. This is America, where the gun is what guarantees your freedom or threatens to take it away. Why would any US citizen consider surrendering this right?

Imagine

Imagine a movie about a group of well-armed law enforcement operatives, consisting of recently discharged military veterans and criminally minded individuals. I'm just asking you to imagine it. We already have an insurgent army dressed like soldiers calling themselves law enforcement. They also dress like criminals while identifying themselves as undercover to the public. This army of law enforcement is well-trained, well-armed, and well-equipped to protect themselves from criminals and the public.

Imagine these police forces simultaneously executing a patriotic act against individual state governments by attacking and terrorizing the lives and extorting resources of the people. Today our law enforcement agencies more closely resemble military special operations forces deployed around the world using the same weapons, equipment, and tactics as our military uses against other organized armies and insurgent terrorists. The actual threat that law enforcement faces should remind us of the search for weapons of mass destruction in Iraq. Yes, there are some dangers to the public in this perpetrated hoax of public safety.

Western movies have certainly helped to change our attitude about acceptance of others. America went to war with itself over whether anyone could be the owner of another human being in a free country, considering the economic and social impact of the loss of forced free labor if slavery was abolished. A change was coming then just like now. You can feel it all around. Our government representatives changed the name of the practice of slavery to criminal punishment in the 13th Amendment. And the states have been exploiting this loophole in the law for profit ever since. We're at war with ourselves today and that makes each citizen venerable to attack, inside our borders by the people we trust to keep the peace.

When you watch Western's, you know that it's easy for bad guys to establish themselves as law enforcement, settle into and take over towns inhabited by frightened defenseless people. Sometimes it would be a sociopath strongman character, most of the time it was just a gang with badges hired and controlled by corrupt officials, or greedy ruthless rich people at the root of the problem. You know a community of neighbors and strangers standing up could cause an immediate change. It only takes one person to do something. Given what we know from movies it's often a disenchanted veteran that feels obligated by oath to stand up to injustice. In the western's everybody bends the rule of law a little. Everyone was pretending to walk a straight line, while judging others for straying. After the civil war all of the states became members of the new USA in which former slaves were declared to have some measure of citizenship. If this were not true, why would the equal rights amendments and voting rights acts be necessary? I wish there were more movies about Negro migration across the west after the civil war. Wouldn't you love to hear the intimate dialog created for the proud people who rose above their previous station, emerging triumphantly over adversity and respected as equals by their neighbors? Successful stories of African American pioneers, building communities in the wilderness with their own hands. In the westerns, we don't see stories of other Americans having trouble in predominantly Negro towns. There can only be three answers: One – There were no Negro towns out west before or after the civil war. Two – Newly emancipated Americans of a certain racial disposition were hindered from prospering across the west during the great expansion. Three – Hollywood excluded their stories.

It's difficult to tell a story of success when it's actually a story of control by obstruction. This is our American experience. Most African Americans don't want to be anything other than American. The media wants you to remember where your ancestors came from so you can understand our station. To that I say, my DNA may have originated from pre-diaspora sub-Saharan African, but it also contains a significant amount of European DNA that has been intertwined here for at least four hundred years. Insects, fish, snakes, plants, and human beings and other aggressive invasive species thrive when their initial appearance is uninhibited by the established occupants of an environment regardless of how they arrive. Resilient species adapt to environmental changes quickly, but only humans have choices. Great effort has been invested in convincing you that African Americans can be competent enough to protect defenseless people around the world, but incompetent to protect themselves at home. Good guys and bad guys. If we can look around the world and see that defenseless people are mistreated everywhere, then we know that new gun control laws are not the answer to poverty, crime, or safety here. Our civil liberties and human rights shouldn't vary so much from state to state because the constitution is the law of the Union. Are we one country or fifty countries loosely held together by a convoluted agreement too complicated for anyone to understand?

Talk to each other, ask yourself some questions. What is your chance of becoming a victim of violent crime, robbery, battery, rape, or murder? What is the number of law enforcement officers, killed per year where you live? What is the number of officer misconduct complaints and officer involved fatalities where you live? How many people live where you live? How many police officers work in your state, city, and town? Include all law enforcement and security agencies. If you have had any of the above referenced crimes committed against you, you might consider being armed. They are! And so is everyone else looking to do you harm according to the police. Please stop getting all of your information from corporate news and electronic social media. Talk to your friends, family, neighbors, and people who disagree with you. There are nightly reports from victims in our war-torn cities. A lot of you feel afraid because of things you've been told, not what you've witnessed or experienced. Seeing it on TV doesn't make you a witness or a victim. It should make you aware that if you live in a city of a million or more and one person is killed every day, your city is not dangerous, do the math. Stop listening to those whose job it is to excite and entertain you. Maybe, you can't imagine civil order collapsing into genocide today. But history cautions us.

We haven't really seen a gun battle between the police and the people. But there have been standoffs throughout our history, most recently between wealthy property owners and federal law enforcement officers during a dispute, over grazing rights on government land. Maybe, after a few million people have been sufficiently intimidated by law enforcement they can relax. Everyone knows that when you can't tell the good guys from the bad guys you need to protect yourself. Too many government officials have been accused and convicted of crimes. The devastation levied on citizens can't be acceptable collateral damage, by us, the government or the media. Sure, the media says stop the gun violence on the news, right after the latest episode of heavily armed and excessively violent, law and order propaganda police TV shows and movies.

Look at your answers to the above questions. Does it really take body armor, high power weapons and large capacity magazines to issue you a traffic citation, respond to an emergency or investigate a crime where you live? The police, unlike our military services, are civilian organizations paid to assist state and local governments, maintain order, assist the public during emergencies, investigate reports of crime, and deliver those accused of crime to the court for justice. It is my personal belief that we can't trust the police until the police trust us. Imagine that.

Why should you trust the media to address your interests and rights?

Top story on the nightly news: Guns, niggers with guns, police with guns, and what to do about niggers with guns without disarming white people or the police. Right after tonight's episode of Badass Badges USA. America has never been safe for Negros, immigrants, or poor people. Let's just be clear about that. Being compliant is not the same as being free.

Whenever an incidence of criminal activity occurs resulting in fatalities, the media goes into the heart of the most disenfranchised areas where the police, criminals, and the citizens have been engaged in an uncivil war forever, to ask the residents if it's dangerous there. Then the media presents the pain of distraught victims as a plea for more gun control. The people need to take control of their own safety. Yes, there will be a brief rise in the number of firearm related injuries and fatalities, but not as many deaths as caused by distracted driving related vehicle collisions each year. Anywhere there's a lot of police activity, it is dangerous.

When the media talks about black-on-black crime it mostly excludes the fact that African Americans are not manufacturing any weapons in the US or anywhere else. When you feed someone poison, don't be surprised when they die from it. This is true with everything manufactured in the US and consumed by African Americans. Cars, guns, drugs, and everything else, we don't make any of them, but we're blamed for their misuse. Illegal for us, manufactured and sold to us by everyone else around the world. You can't get ahead by being a consumer of everyone else's products. Food for thought! Share this with everyone you know.

Celebrities can afford an entourage of armed protection and live in exclusive gated communities while speaking out about the effect of gun violence. No guns allowed. Stop the killing. This is their mantra and call for action. I wonder if the security personnel and police officers hired for their events are unarmed.

The media doesn't mention that. The media reported that the police and government will launch investigations to understand what happened and use this data to prevent recurrence. But they're not very good at preventing any crime. Guns can't be the problem because every police officer that arrives on scene has at least one gun on their person for their personal protection. Millions of US citizens are responsible firearms owners, and these restrictions and prohibitions defy science and the constitution. The media hasn't attempted to show citizens as responsible firearm owners or that firearms have many safe and legitimate uses other than hunting.

No media outlet elaborates on why the police always arrive after the deadly part of the terror incident is over. And the media has the audacity to label the police, "First Responders", as if the people on the scene providing first aid assistance to the victims and information to the police, emergency medical personnel, and media's reporters, are irrelevant. Armed people do a great job of protecting themselves. Ask the Police.

When a group of armed people requires you to surrender your arms, they intend to control you. These so-called disturbed mass killers, domestic terrorists, and street gang members are not so crazy or dedicated to their cause or agenda, as to go to police stations to shoot up a building full of armed individuals. Stop making excuses for, and celebrities out of America's domestic terrorists, monsters, and killers. What's the difference between killing people for fanatical religious beliefs, vanity, insanity, or control? For defenseless, naïve, unsuspecting, terrorized and dead people the result is the same. The perpetrators are instantly immortalized, and the police exalted to hero status by the media hounds chasing ratings for product sponsors. That's not to say or pretend that the police are not a vital part of our civil order.

Unarmed civilians subdued a shooter on a college campus in Seattle and held him for police. The police arrived in full force and battle gear after the incident was over. But the police looked very impressive on video as "First Responders". The daily news makes mass murderers in America look like simply mentally ill people, and suicide attackers anywhere else look like vicious murderous terrorists. This is why the media and government promote gun control for law abiding citizens. Each broadcast ends with law enforcement officials assuring us that everything is under control. Yet, there's new crimes and new villains every day. Crime is not under control, we are!

Challenge Eight

Niggas Ltd. is proud to announce expansion of Niggas Training Center (NTC) to the general public in our new environmentally friendly facilities to be opened around the country. NTC offers, a comprehensive firearms educational experience using the most advance simulator technology to help you become a responsible Nigga, Bitch, or Bastard owner. In an effort to address the issues and problems associated with the absence of appropriate firearm training in urban areas, we are proud to announce the opening of our first high tech training facility in Chicago, called The Plantation.

The Plantation is a state-of-the-art firearm education and training facility utilizing high tech military surplus firearm training simulators to teach firearm safety, marksmanship and responsibility to the public in urban areas. In America's major metropolitan cities where violent crime is highest, access to quality firearms safety and marksmanship training facilities is limited. The absence of emergency defensive skills training opportunities has rendered our citizens venerable to out of control criminal terrorist activity plaguing communities and the escalation of law enforcement organizations with qualified immunity. Firearms training facilities are community building places where everyone can learn and practice a skill to strengthen our country.

The Plantation will offer the most comprehensive firearm safety and marksmanship training available outside of the US military. Students will be guided by military trained firearm experts called Masters and Overseers providing hands on instruction to help students achieve state required training for a concealed carry license (CCL). On the Plantation you will learn:

- Laws regarding ownership, possession, proper use and handling of your Niggas, Bitches, and Bastards
- Safety and proper care of your Niggas, Bitches, and Bastards
- Legal sale or transfer of your Niggas, Bitches, and Bastards
- Prohibited use of Niggas, Bitches, and Bastards
- What to do if your Niggas, Bitches, or Bastards are lost or stolen
- Appropriate methods of transporting your Niggas, Bitches, and Bastards
- Appropriate papers to carry when transporting or shipping your Niggas, Bitches, and Bastards

The Plantation masters and overseers will guide you through the rigorous process of learning to use your Niggas, Bitches, Bastards, or other legally owned firearms in a safe controlled environment without the use of live ammunition. Upon successful completion of your training, you will be qualified to apply for a CCL in all 50 states. As a member of The Plantation, you can bring your Niggas and Bitches with you. Access to ranges, technical consultants, recreational facilities and other services are included in your membership fee.

Arming other countries

In solidarity with struggling democracies around the world today, some of our most outspoken gun control elected officials are in favor of arming the civilian populations of foreign countries so those people can protect themselves. Yet here, where thousands of lives and billions of dollars in personal property are lost to crime every year, the only plan our elected representatives can offer is more control over law abiding citizens with ever more restrictive self-defense and personal protection laws.

At the same time, law enforcement and revenue collection agencies have been given real military equipment and more invasive powers of surveillance and detention of US citizens, as crimes continue to escalate. The rise in crime is directly related to economics, corporate greed, government greed and corruption, proliferation of laws, and voluntary surrender of rights and abdication of individual responsibilities in the name of public safety. And what have we received in return? Answer: the highest homicide, suicide, and incarceration rates in the wealthiest economy on earth.

We've all seen images of defenseless people being abused by gangs, terrorists, police, armies, and oppressive governments around the world. This is the age of information and global connection. Images of atrocities in Europe, Asia, Africa, Australia, and the Americas during the 20th and 21st centuries, inflames our sensibilities as free people to the point of offering the lives of our children for these defenseless people. We want them to have a fighting chance against overwhelming odds while many popular media influencers are promoting this concept that armed citizens, especially armed African Americans, are frightening to them and it should be illegal.

We gave Israel nuclear weapons to defend itself from its neighbors. We gave the people of Iraq and Afghanistan advanced weapons to free themselves from communist control. We maintain a standing army in South Korea to protect them from their unpredictable neighbors. Our government officials, law enforcement agencies, and religious leaders want you to be convinced that by prohibiting your right to self-protection, you can trust them to protect you and your loved ones from anyone doing you harm. Social media has been used as a tool of misinformation regarding intimidation by the law enforcement. Police officials say most of their officers are very good at doing their thing, so the public should be afraid of them. The media and the government advocate that something should be done to further restrict your access to arms for self-defense.

Why maintain and demand your right to keep and bear arms

Some people believe that the police should be armed greater than you, because they encounter dangerous situations as a part of their daily activity. They ignore the fact that unarmed defenseless people are the victims of crime and witnesses to dangerous encounters with armed individuals, criminals and police, every day. Our lives are in danger every day. Are the police calling you when they encounter trouble? You and I have a greater potential for a deadly criminal encounter than any uniformed police officer or armed individual at any time of day or night.

Violent crimes don't happen to people in a predictable way. Or do they? In the movies the bad people insert themselves into a situation. They assess the intended victim and attack without warning or consideration for victim safety. Have you ever seen a movie where the good guy has time, opportunity, and presence of mind in a deadly, emergency situation, retreat from the danger, go to their vehicle, unlock the trunk, retrieve a locked container, open it, get an unloaded firearm, load it, return to the dangerous situation and thwart the bad guy's criminal intent? In the movies, super-cops and superheroes can do anything, and be everywhere, but just imagine you doing it. The United States of Confusion is that what we've become in the age of artificial intelligence.

Defenseless people are always at the mercy of bullies, tyrants, and criminals. Our constitution guarantees every citizen the power to resist oppression and terrorism. We welcome the support of law enforcement, but it's usually too late for the victims when the police arrive.

A veteran, in Chicago, armed with a handgun protected his family by shooting a dangerous perpetrator who attacked them on their property. This is what self-defense is all about. Imagine a woman walking down a residential neighborhood street in the middle of the day, distracted in her mobile technology, when criminal perpetrators approach her by car. Imagine the distracted woman's surprise when the car suddenly stops, cutting off her path. The perpetrators exit the vehicle and rob the distracted law-abiding citizen at gun point. Even the threat of being armed, real or ruse, can be a powerful tool to perpetrate or deter attacks on individuals. I believe one of the reasons police treat citizens the way they do is because they expect an uneducated public to obey them out of fear. Law enforcement agencies rob us of our rights every day under the threat of abuse and murder, expecting us to believe that they, the police, make citizens safe! Like a pimp.

Why trust historical Black institutions

It hurts the advancement of people of color when organizations that have traditionally been thought of as our guardians would support any of the current gun control laws or any of the laws that give law enforcement officers autonomy over citizens. The mainstream civil rights organizations continue to support a position that Negros with guns are dangerous to themselves and need to earn our rights through patience and permission from the government. Other than the 2nd Amendment right, what other right do these organizations support law abiding citizens having to get permission to exercise? I imagine most members of these organizations are learned and honorable individuals, so I'm confused. Pardon my ignorance. What I hear from African American elected officials at all levels of government in California is their support for disarming everyone except for police and privileged individuals. If you own or have a firearm accessible to you, these organizations consider you a potential criminal and must be disarmed for public safety. These so-called sensible gun control laws are being passed around like a giant joint of cannabis. Makes sense when you're smoking it, but none of these laws have stopped crime or been proven any better for our safety than the straightforward instruction to our representatives in the 2nd Amendment. Many of these organizations either agree or are silent about cosmetic changes to policing, instead of addressing the abuse of thousands of police authority and protection laws in exchange for common sense law enforcement. I fully support your 5th Amendment right to remain silent. Like so many of our elected representatives today these organization are more focused on the rights of illegal immigrants than the rights of disenfranchised Americans.

Challenge Nine

Niggas Ltd. is proud to announce, revolutionary ammunition for all of our Niggas and Bitches. The new ammo will be called: Ho's. Ho's will come in sizes to fit all of our Niggas and Bitches. What makes Ho's revolutionary is that they are capable of penetrating fabric and flesh like any conventional bullet but will disintegrate on contact with any hard surface, minimizing collateral damage.

Ammunition that disintegrates on contact with hard surfaces will reduce the chances of injuring people when bullets don't strike their intended targets. The neighborhood can rest easy knowing that a Ho will not break into your home in the middle of the night to hurt your children from neighbors trying to save their own. But a Ho can stop an intruder when lethal protection is required. Ho's will be made from a secret scientifically developed biodegradable compound that remains in a solid projectile state until it strikes a solid surface such as a wall, door, or body armor.

Get you Nigga or Bitch loaded with a couple of Ho's, and you'll be ready for whatever comes your way. You don't have to worry about a stray Ho hurting anyone. A Ho may not break a window if one gets away from you, but a Ho will get under the skin of any perpetrator that comes between you and your safety. Warning: Firing a Ho can be lethal.

Law Enforcement

If you live in a country where the people who enforce the law operate with different laws than all other citizens, you are a subject, not a citizen. Americans should understand that the organizations that we label as police or law enforcement were crated to serve and protect the wealthy and their assets, not to serve and protect the people. Police agencies evolved from slave catchers into the urban soldiers we know today is the history of law enforcement for African Americans. The name has changed but the practice remains the same.

The general public has been misled by the government, special interest, and media groups to believe that the National Rifle Association (NRA) has the power to change the law. It doesn't. Contrary to this popular belief, the advocacy of the NRA doesn't compare to the power and influence the FOP has over our elected officials at every level of government. The Fraternal Order of Police is the most powerful gun lobby in the United States. This police union and law enforcement lobbying agency is so powerful that it forced our government to create special laws that apply to only FOP members for their protection and authority. FOP members are unimpeded by individual state gun control laws imposed on all other citizens, including our active-duty military members and veterans.

Law enforcement officers regardless of their duty status (On duty, off duty, furloughed, suspended, retired, fired, or working part-time for private security agencies), can purchase the most lethal weapons in any state over the counter without waiting periods, background checks, or state issued concealed carry permits. They can purchase guns and ammunition together right on the spot, including fully automatic military weapons, explosives, and body armor, right over the counter. Law enforcement officers can have guns in their possession that are not registered to an officer or department, even if it's connected to a crime. At the same time, the FOP lobbies congress to restrict and prohibit law abiding citizen's constitutional right to self-defense. The FOP continues to block reciprocity laws for you and fights to guarantee the ability of their members to be armed and protected by law at all times. The FOP fights to keep you under their control.

On the surface this might sound like a reasonable privilege for people sworn to protect you. On closer examination you'll discover that in 2005 the FOP forced the US Supreme Court to reiterate that the police, law enforcement, or peace officers are not responsible for your personal safety or the security of your property. At the same time, guaranteeing members of the FOP the right to protect themselves behind the shield of assumed qualified immunity mostly free from prosecution and personal responsibility for individual and agency misconduct through law and the Grand Jury process. Food for thought, recent televised events have demonstrated that apparently these well-trained FOP members are not very good at preventing attacks on Americans and that they have become part of the growing terror threat to at least African Americans. The FOP has instigated changes to our laws in a language even our law makers can't understand and can't explain. But the intolerable behavior of the police and the criminals has only intensified against their common source of resource and revenue: The American people.

Why would you trust law enforcement agencies?

Law enforcement agencies are dependent on the proliferation of crime to justify the immense power and control over us that we have unconsciously but trustingly relinquished to them for our safety. Law enforcement is a big, powerful, and profitable business that uses fear to justify its power, intrusion, and cost, while failing to produce the utopian society, free of crime it promises. Law enforcement agencies, advocates, and unions, constantly lobbies congress to erode your individual rights in the name of public safety while they reign terror across the country.

In your lifetime, how many gunfights have the police lost to the bad guys? In your lifetime, how many times have the police where you live been proven by court records to have been involved and convicted of criminal activities? How many times have law enforcement agencies tried to convince us that these were the actions of rouge officers and not reflective of law enforcement in general? How many times have law enforcement agencies requested and received additional enforcement capabilities without proving that their methods are an effective way to win their war on crime and poverty?

How many elected officials need to be exposed for having armed personal protection, including police protection, concealed carry license, armored vests, armored vehicles, and assault weapons, at our expense, while presenting an anti-gun message to the public? I don't need to name any of them. You know who they are. People in the public trust have continuously demonstrated a propensity for corruption and deception for personal gain, political and physical control of the people. In California, with the most restrictive firearm laws in the nation, stanch proponents of more restrictive firearm laws, have been exposed for having a "Do as I say" philosophy, while protecting themselves with firearms. Ask Nancy Pelosi.

Police charged and convicted of rape, robbery, extortion, prostitution, murder, gang activity, and corruption, gun and drug trafficking, want you to rely on them for your protection and wellbeing. Elected officials charged and convicted of corruption and discrimination, want you to rely on them for leadership. Cities and states have paid astronomical amounts of our tax dollars to victims of law enforcement misconduct without admitting any wrongdoing.

I can't afford a personal bodyguard or armored vehicle. No one is going to pay me and a bunch of my friends to dress up like soldiers and give us guns to drive around their neighborhood making sure everyone is safe inside their homes by breaking into their homes and killing them. No one is going to be happy if I killed someone because of a report of someone's property violation. Or just because I felt my safety was threatened by someone I profiled and approached as a possible criminal before I accosted them. If only they would have followed my commands.

Every time you hear the government is buying something new to keep us safe, remember it's your money. We don't need to buy more stuff for the police to use against us in the game of public safety. Demilitarize the police, institute constitutional carry nationwide, or maybe urban communities should form local militias to circumvent the gun laws throughout the country.

What misdeeds of law enforcement can I tell you about that you can't already see in any crime drama on TV? What happened to these self-proclaimed officers of the court that caused peace officers to be outfitted and armed like soldiers? What adversary do they confront that you and I don't encounter every day without a gun or body armor? Most people don't go looking to be involved in a firearms incident. Every day armed individuals violate your personal space and comfort zone and there's nothing you can do about it. Are you comfortable with this arrangement? Every year defenseless people are the prime victims of violent crime. Each year the number of reported violent crimes against citizens in Chicago is staggering. The number of civilian casualties in this one city is greater than all of the combined crimes perpetrated against all police officers nationwide in a single year. The number of officer-involved shootings are becoming equal to all other shootings in America.

Law enforcement agencies and officers continue to be engaged in unlawful and unnecessarily dangerously risky activities under the guise of catching criminals and enforcing the law. No-knock warrants are designed for civil executions of criminal suspects. You have the right to defend your home from uninvited, unannounced, intruders seeking to do you harm even if the intruders are police. If you unexpectedly knock on the door of any law enforcement officer's home at 0-dark thirty, they are going to arm themselves before answering the door. If you enter their personal space unannounced, expect to be shot. If you break in, expect to be shot. The intruder can't claim self-defense for shooting you while they're in the act of breaking into your property to cause, you harm. That would defy logic and the Constitution. Ask Fred Hampton and Breonna Taylor.

Challenge Ten

Niggas Ltd. is proud to announce a revolutionary new cleaner and lubricant for all, of our Niggas, Bitches, and Bastards. The new cleaner/lubricant will be called: The Juice.

Nobody wants a dirty Nigga, a nasty dry Bitch, or a rusty Bastard. The Juice will help you keep your Niggas clean and trouble free. It will help make your Bitch easier to get loaded and help you jack a load of Shit from your Bastard with smooth one hand pumping action. The Juice will be made from a renewable environmentally friendly biodegradable organic compound that removes dirt from your Nigga's hard and moving parts, lubricates your Bitch's openings, and make your Bastard's pump action load and eject Shit with ease. You can keep The Juice bottled up for life and it will still deliver outstanding performance when you need it. Note: Although Bitches are designed to be self-lubricating, they may require cleaning after firing a Ho.

The Police

Let's be clear, this is not about citizens versus police. The police are an absolute necessity and invaluable element of our social order construct. When the police are assisting the public during emergencies, helping to maintain the peace, investigating crimes after they've been committed and to bring the accused to justice, the police can be very effective! The police are totally ineffective at preventing Americans from mistreating and killing each other or preventing any illegal activity from occurring. Crime prevention is the responsibility of every citizen. We know what it takes to defend our country and ourselves. Ask Alexander Hamilton.

Law enforcement in the form of police officers evolved from slave catchers to protect the interest of the powerful, former outlaw gang members turned sheriff, and developed into small territorial armies commonly known as law enforcement agencies today. The history of westward expansion reminds us that many murderous armed individuals and organized groups put on badges and established themselves as law enforcement and private security organizations. They served powerful private concerns or wealthy individuals paying the most for their brand of law enforcement, while robbing and terrorizing the citizens into their interpretation of safety. The police are not supposed to be our military. They're not supposed to be intimidators, extortionists, executioners, murderers or militia. They are supposed be peace officers and we all are supposed to be civilized. The police and criminals share goals that keep us paying for a false sense of security and real fear. Ever wonder why your neighborhood looks like a prison with bars and plywood on the windows? Or a war zone covered with graffiti murals of the casualties and martyrs of a never-ending war on crime? Do you wonder why hordes of disorderly people are roaming the streets wreaking havoc unimpeded by our uniformed army of dedicated public servants working to enforce the law on us?

The police are always too late for the victims, always on time for the cameras. With training and a few thousand dollars in equipment, you too could feel as safe as any police officer. People trained in firearm care, use, and responsibility are of no more danger to the police or the public than any individual police officer is a danger to you.

The Supreme Court of the United States ruled that police officers do not have a constitutional duty to protect any individual citizen from potential harm. Police are people with guns. Don't be confused about why they want you unarmed and under their control. Serve and protect, is just a slogan like the inscription on the base of the Statue of Liberty. Americans should be demanding an immediate reduction of police powers and protections everywhere. Or at least the public should have some detailed instructions and procedures as rules of engagement between citizens and law enforcement personnel so that everyone has the same rules. What's the difference between being detained and being arrested, don't they feel the same in handcuffs? The right to remain silent can't be our only right when we encounter rouge police officers. These rules should apply also to witnesses because of what happens to good citizens in court. Americans are supposed to have presumed innocence! That means unless the police are in direct pursuit or an eyewitness, they shouldn't assume that you are guilty of anything. Currently, you only have to be suspected of a potential crime by any individual law enforcement officer at any time or place for the police to exercise authority to accost you. A hunch, a feeling, a suspicion, any police officer can circumvent your civil rights, accost, search, seize property, and detain you at gun point based on this concept of evidence. If you're Black and armed, you can be executed on the spot for officers' safety. Ask the FOP.

Our laws must be too complicated for the average African American. We keep doing the same things and expecting different results because of how the law is explained and applied to us. Looking to the government for protection and reform hasn't worked. Most of our government officials, especially at the local level, are just managers of the public trust and resources. They don't have to be leaders. The government can't legislate, a cure for our culture of waiting for someone else to behave responsibly, expecting others to change their behavior, without anyone doing anything different. The police have committed so many atrocities against Negro citizens under the color of law throughout our history that many of us don't believe police commit crime until we learn about it from the media.

Clubs, knives, dogs, and guns are the most common and most effective means of self-defense and deterrence to physical assault known to people around the world. No law enforcement officer, criminal, affluent person, or soldier is going to confront people wanting to do them harm without these basic tools. Even a Neanderthal understood that a defenseless being would be subjected to mistreatment by armed humans. But clubs, knives, spears, arrows, and dogs are no match for guns. Ask any police officer.

Today, the police that patrol minority communities behave and dress more like soldiers in occupied territory than peace officers. And why shouldn't they, our country is not safe for us, or should I say that is image of America in the media. There is not much news in communities of collective civility. The police have admitted and demonstrated that they cannot protect us from crime, each other, or from them. Law enforcement officials believe that if only select civilians are allowed to possess firearms all of us will be safer and that would make police work so much easier. And they're correct, aren't they? Police officers and select civilians would feel safer! Why is it that constitutional carry states have dramatically lower rates of burglary, robbery, battery, rape, and homicide than states where the right to self-protection is severely restricted?

Our police look, dress, and act like quasi military security squads of movie warlords under the control of a Hollywood dictator. Some special police units dress and behave like the criminals they're supposed to be apprehending. Some of them have been exposed for participating in blatant criminal activities including drugs, human trafficking, guns and murder. How safe do you feel now? The police spend too much of our resources on revenue collection. We have militarized a police army for the purpose of tax, fees, fines, and interest collection. When you are not allowed to protect yourself or defend your property it's easy to be intimidated into submission.

I don't pretend to know the ins and outs complexity of law enforcement agencies or criminal enterprises. I'm just a US citizen living in a war-torn country, rendered defenseless by state and local laws designed to keep me a victim of the two warring factions (police and criminals). How can any US citizen realize the American dream when we are ruled by hypnotists, mystics, magicians, swindlers, and bullies in an elitist culture that makes us glorify the illusion? I believe it is reasonable and possible for a police officer to engage you without asserting imminent power over you. Today, it's difficult for most of us to identify the good guys from the bad guys when we encounter police. Civility requires citizens to cooperate with law enforcement. You are not required to obey the police without question or reason. Americans surrender to the police because we believe in the presumption of innocence.

One person is no match for a group of well-trained police officers. We see that every day in the corporate news and on social media. Every day unarmed citizens are fatally shot during routine encounters with police. You encounter police and bad people on both sides of crime, during and after. Your money, car, smart phone, computer, bicycle, purse, body, children, and your life are being taken by both groups like extortionists collecting protection fees from little bodega owners in the big city. Do you feel safe?

I believe that state and local law enforcement officers should never be under cover and should only be armed with small caliber, limited capacity official handguns which are checked-in after each shift. During their off-duty hours they should only be allowed the same level of personal protection as all other law-abiding citizens. But they can't even imagine this. The news media would paint anyone suggesting such a change to our totalitarian law enforcement agencies as delusional or subversive. But you don't see the street gangs or the crazies shooting up police stations or media facilities. When police officers will not leave their homes without being armed, will not live in the communities they work in, and require that you be unarmed, you live in a police state, not a free state!

The cost of our safety could be reduced by reducing the number of police vehicles in metropolitan areas. The police could use public transportation for all routine and non-emergency responsibilities. Police officers should be required to live in the city where they work. And train all police that they should expect every US citizen to be legally armed. They already treat us like we're illegally armed, at least that's what they say.

Still behaving like fifty individual countries, state governments and local law enforcement have a demonstrated disdain for and defiance of federal laws. Police across this country are responsible for killing too many unarmed people for us to trust them with our safety or protection today. Police abuse seems more blatant and frequent today because they're on video looking and behaving like soldiers, gangsters and thugs, and getting away with it. African Americans have been reporting this forever.

The police are not encountering armies shooting up shopping malls, schools, or public events. And many police officers are members of civilian para-military militias groups capable of military style operations against civilian populations. Any governor, mayor, or local sheriff can unleash these little armies on us at any time. It has happened repeatedly in this country.

The police have access to real military equipment, military tactical training techniques, and other, strictly military intelligence. The US military is not officially performing joint urban environment operations exercises with civilian law enforcement agencies. However, our state National Guard units are officially sharing military equipment, surveillance techniques, manned aircraft, unmanned drones, secret satellites, armored vehicles, firearms, information and tactics with civilian police departments. Our military is not preparing for any defense against police attacks on civilians. They have no system for tracking and monitoring service members who are members of civilian law enforcement agencies, private security organizations, or militia groups.

Yes, the police look very impressive on the evening news in high definition. But you've never seen these law enforcement agencies in action against a real army of trained individuals who are not afraid of them. Don't be confused. Law enforcement agencies have made an industry out of our fear of the police. Something must change. If you want someone to treat you differently, then you must behave differently. America must de-militarize the police and stop the erosion of human rights in America. Crimes reported to the police cannot be prevented because they have already occurred. The police depend on you to identify the crime and the parties responsible. You and I don't go looking for criminal activity. We have the potential for deadly encounters 24 hours a day in the form of criminals and police whether at home or on the street. In fact, every time we encounter a police officer, it is an armed encounter. Being armed can't be a crime in the US. I'm not an advocate for anyone to be armed or for violence against any group or person. I don't believe that being prepared to defend yourself from anyone doing you harm is a crime.

Government reports reveal that the majority of citizens surrender to law enforcement without incidence or resistance. That includes armed citizens with outstanding arrest warrants driving under the influence. Some people run from the police, fleeing for their lives. People have good cause for running from the police as evidenced by officer-involved shootings of fleeing unarmed suspects. Remember those images of police attending lynchings, beatings, tear gassings, fire-hosing, bombings, shootings, and vicious police dog attacks on unarmed defenseless people pleading for equality under the law. If you take enough pictures, you're bound to capture a bad one on occasion, just doing routine police work. Police intimidate each other into misrepresenting events to the media, the public and the court. Denying citizens' rights through lies, propaganda, intimidation, and force is supposed to be illegal.

If the police can look and behave like soldiers or criminals, or anything that doesn't look like a police officer can we be safe from them? Domestic terrorists, known criminals, covert military insurgents, and police could be hiding among the homeless on our streets in tent cities popping up all over our major cities. These people are in your face every day asking for money, assaulting and robbing civilians, breaking into vehicles and homes, taking what they want from you. The police admit to disguising themselves as homeless people, drug addicts, prostitutes, game show hosts, teachers, executives and gang members. Assistance is the service that we buy from police agencies, but we're not getting what we pay for. The police are incapable of preventing free people from committing crime against each other. The police want you to believe that they're special when they show up to do the job, we pay them for. That somehow, they're at greater risk of harm than you. Why do we keep asking for more police and are willing to pay more for a service that doesn't work?

The police have been involved in every kind of illegal activity you can imagine, including murder of people in their custody. Now looking like an army, the police want to claim that they are making us safer by disarming citizens who have not committed any crime. The police need to come out of the military tactics and uniforms and focus their efforts on the job they're hired to perform. Crime prevention is the responsibility of every citizen. Yes, shootings in self-defense may increase for a short period because the police will insist on confrontation for control of the people and revenue under their jurisdiction. The police consider any move you make as a threat against them, and they have a right to defend themselves with deadly force. The criminals see you as low hanging fruit, easy picking. This is part of the problem.

How can anyone know when they're breaking the law? Every new law gives the police more authority to stop, search, and detain you, without having to inform you of any violation. The officer may not know the law they allege you're violating. This is nothing new for African Americans. Police want you to believe we pay them to put themselves in harm's way. So, they practice armed confrontation, detainment, interrogation, confiscation, and forfeiture with the public every day. Putting everyone else in harm's way, while trying to convince us that we're safer, being protected by them. The ability and responsibility to protect and defend yourself is your human right. Being controlled by police in the name of public safety is not safe. Americans are citizens, not subjects of the government like the people of Australia, Canada, or England. The police have proven that they are only capable of protecting themselves. Police departments chasing the most money and paying their officers the most produce the smallest results in crime reduction. Law enforcement agencies trade officers between jurisdictions like athletes in a franchise sports league, raking in huge profits from the public without a winning season on record. More police and more laws are not the answer to crime in America. The law enforcement system has turned into an industry that just like the cost of the occupation of Iraq and Afghanistan, we can no longer afford.

Challenge Eleven

Because of changing rules and regulations regarding firearm ownership, Niggas Ltd. is introducing firearm insurance to provide you with peace of mind for all of your Niggas, Bitches, and Bastards. The company will be called: Salvation Insurance Co.

In the event that one of your Niggas, Bitches, or Bastards is involved in a shooting injury or death of anyone, Salvation Insurance may be there to misrepresent you against any legitimate claim. Our crack team of over unqualified insurance adjusters and attorneys will keep the plaintiff bogged down in irrelevant bureaucratic procedures and incomplete paperwork until an incompetent attorney can be retained at your expense. Insure as many Niggas, Bitches, or Bastards as you own for the price of one. It is not about how many Niggas you own, but how you use them. Salvation Insurance will replace any lost or stolen Nigga, Bitch, or Bastard included on your unwritten policy. You've been waiting for Salvation, now it's here. Should you ever have to use your Niggas, Bitches, or Bastards to defend yourself, pray that Salvation Insurance may be there to defend, you.

Police Service Weapons

When the standard issue sidearm service weapon for law enforcement officers was a six-shot revolver, no suspect was ever shot sixteen times by a single officer. Police should not have any weapons that the public can't have. That includes military issue weapons with high-capacity magazines. Police are people with guns engaged in a pseudo-military terrorist assault exercise against US citizens daily under the guise of public safety. Ask your local police department to have their officers to patrol your neighborhood unarmed accompanied only by a well-trained law enforcement canine. The police are not going to rely on just a dog when they encounter you. Just like you, that dog doesn't know what law you may have broken. And that police officer believes that dog's life is more valuable than yours.

Dallas, Texas 2016, an American veteran of the war in Afghanistan, allegedly perpetrated an unprovoked deliberate assault on the uniformed police officers during a demonstration against deadly attacks on unarmed Americans by police officers nationwide. A police union spokesperson described the culture on the streets of America as being in a war zone. The weapon used by the aggrieved veteran that wounded seven and killed five well trained and military equipped uniformed police officers was a more than 70-year-old, WWII era Soviet made SKS, ten shot, semi-automatic rifle. While the police decry the lethality of this California compliant rifle, they fail to inform the public that this weapon, functionally and ergonomically no match for the modern military equipment used by the police department.

The Dallas Police Chief praised the courage of his officers for using a military robot equipped with a camera and a bomb to kill the surrounded and trapped veteran. A bomb! And the police say they're out gunned! The public to date has not seen the video of what happened to this veteran in his final moments of life. Does anyone remember the Black Liberation Organization MOVE? In 1985, the city of Philadelphia police used a bomb to extricate the group from a residential building and burned down the neighborhood. That police action killed eleven people, made over two hundred people homeless, terrorizes citizens to this day, and cost the people millions of dollars in the aftermath. Tell me that you are not afraid of the police, and I'll show you a very privileged person, you.

We have the US military and the National Guard in every state to address emergencies, disasters, insurrection, boarder encroachment, and foreign military enemy attacks. Cameras and vehicle registration can enforce traffic violations. That would leave the police free to perform peacekeeping, emergency assistance and bring wanted individuals to justice. It is widely advertised that more technology leads to efficiency, reduction in evidence error and risk of human injury. Checkout your local bank, more technology, fewer employee errors to worry about, better service for you. Every industry is right sizing with technology except for law enforcement. Checkout those bank fees and executive salaries, technology making it easier. As revenue collection agencies, police departments are very efficient. Even with new technology and additional officers, police have proven that they cannot prevent crime from occurring in a free society. You can't force free people to feel safe.

The military could stop the gang problem right now. But we have a problem. Americans have been allowing their police to look and act like soldiers and gang members. Can you imagine the military cooperating with a partner that is easily corrupted by money and power and is known to be part of the problem? Ask Dick Chaney. Let the military fight the terrorists and gangs in America. Gang wars would stop immediately. You can laugh now. Ask the Army about Mogadishu.

Challenge Twelve

Nigga Ltd. in response to law enforcement agencies recommendations for limited capacity magazines for handguns, we are introducing our first Simi-automatic pistol: The Lord. The Lord is the first Simi-automation handgun manufactured by Niggas Ltd. The Lord will be available in .45APC, 44 magnum and .50 caliber with a three-round capacity magazine. The single stack trinity magazine holds only three rounds. Its slim profile keeps the Lord invisible until you need protection. Made in the US from stainless American steel with advance artificial intelligence user recognition technology, that prevents use by anyone other than the registered and programed operator.

The Lord is the perfect companion for both law enforcement and civilians who desire the most powerful intervention to stop evil doers. The large caliber design delivers biblical proportions of righteous stopping power when you find yourself in the valley of the shadow of crime and mayhem. The Lord will provide the faithful with a fighting chance for survival and salvation.

When you have the Lord with you, you'll have nothing to fear. You can have faith in the Lord, and the Lord is a redeemer that will deliver a lethal dose of righteousness for your protection. The Lord will be there when you can't make it by yourself. You can tell everyone the Lord is with you all the time. You'll feel comforted having the Lord with you. You'll want to testify about what the Lord has done for you. You can rest easy with the Lord. The Lord will protect you, your family and property when no help is available. The Lord can save you when all hope is gone. Ask and you shall be given Salvation Insurance at no cost. It provides bail bond for up to $500,000 secured by you, and initial confession legal counseling in the event of an incident involving your use of the Lord.

Mass Shootings

We all grieve with everyone wanting the senseless shootings to stop. Willful people are deliberate. Stupid people will do things that baffle them. Angry people will do things they regret. It is almost impossible to defend yourself from an attack with your mobile device and hope for salvation. More restrictive laws on law abiding citizens can't be the only way to address domestic terrorism, criminal acts, or mental instability. We will have law enforcement, even if it kills you. People, friends and families of the victims, just like those of fallen officers want something to make them feel safe again. Restricting freedom is not the answer.

Every law enforcement officer that responds to mass shooting incidents arrives armed with the same weapons and tactics as the army. They arrived in armored vehicles and combat attire, too late for any of the victims. But they do look very formidable on my multi-media streaming devices, restoring order and gathering evidence on how well they performed. Don't be confused. The sight of combat soldiers disguised as police is terrorizing and traumatizing to children who play virtual combat game on multi-media devices and watch terrorist attacks in their neighborhoods from the windows of their homes and on the nightly news. Every mass shooting was perpetrated by willful individuals with deliberate intentions to harm others. We make up excuses for the assailant's behavior to justify acceptance of more restrictions out of our own fear. Arming yourself to kill human beings except in self-defense should be a crime.

In what the media calls mass shooting incidence in the United States, most of these assailants reportedly terminate themselves before they could be arrested according to the police and the news media. At each of these incidences more than a hundred military equipped law enforcement officers arrived on site. And every police department nationwide goes on high alert status. Why? What all these incidences have in common is they occur in places where people are not expected to be armed or where firearms are prohibited. These unarmed defenseless people were targeted and murdered before the police arrived. The police did what they do best: Respond after a crime has been committed and reported. Yes, sometimes an officer is killed in the performance of what they believe is their duty. I'm sure law enforcement agencies analyze data collected regarding an officer's contributing actions that results in any injury or fatality. The officer's ego, privilege, and assumed authority have been reported as factors in officer involved shootings. Safety and crime prevention is every citizen's responsibility. Your individual safety is your personal responsibility. Ask any insurance company.

The police and the news media do a great job of making you feel helpless, and the police look like a shield of fearless heroes when the shooting is over and all that's left to do is collect the bodies. All those people were already dead or injured, and the perpetrators had escaped, died, or gave up by the time the police and media arrive.

Unarmed citizens without the aid of law enforcement officers subdued and disarmed a deranged terrorist and detained him while waiting for the police to arrive. I mean the first responders to arrive. You may wonder what kind of psychotropic medications these individuals are on who consciously terrorize and murder defenseless people. The experts analyze the information provided by the law enforcement to predict the end of the crime. Don't be confused. Because without the public, law enforcement couldn't solve a homicide committed by a police officer on video, surrounded by an army of police officers and civilian eyewitnesses. Ask Rohm Emmanuel. The only place police encounter massive armed gangs is in movies and on television. All these mass shootings occurred where the assailants believed the victims were helpless.

In Dallas, it seems that the police and the media's rush to provide some explanation for the confrontation purposely demonized this veteran. He was trained to be effective at protecting American interests overseas. He returned home to constant news reports of defenseless people being terrorized and murdered by a clearly identifiable heavily armed group, the police. When the police and the media say that this veteran served in the US Army as part of an engineering battalion the public is misinformed to think that he was not in a combat role or that he was in an office somewhere out of harm's way making drawings. Remember the military reduced its common skills training in favor of highly specialized fighting forces including engineering battalions. This soldier was exposed to danger just as any other combat troop during deployment. The media and the police have exaggerated the importance of his possession of military training materials found at his home. Most veterans maintain some interest in military tactics and equipment before and after their service. That too is being used by the police and the media to demonize this veteran. No one is mentioning that he may have learned the shoot and move techniques not only from military training, but from hours of playing obscenely violent virtual reality urban combat simulation video games that millions of young people play every day. If mental health professionals recognize violent video games perceived impact on crime and policing, then shouldn't that be considered? Freedom fighters don't always do the right thing, but this is an armed conflict, and causalities have occurred for combatants and bystanders. I don't justify his actions, but I can understand that a lie has been exposed in the killing of more unarmed Americans by police.

The police, after using a high-tech military robot equipped with a camera, microphone, and a bomb have not let the public hear or see what happened prior to detonating the bomb that killed the suspect. Instead of objective evidence the public was offered hearsay as fact. Something is not right with this picture or lack of pictures. Could it be that because he attacked and killed several members of the law enforcement family, that the police decided they were not about to let the courts prolong his existence another day? Justice is swift in the hands of the police when one of theirs is harmed. The Dallas Police chief said that he would use the robot and bomb again to save his officers lives. Talk about wild, wild, west! Every police officer showed up with at least one gun to defend them-selves and to attack the suspect. Maybe he was a frustrated patriot, war veteran, tired of seeing unarmed people attacked and killed by these uniformed cult members disguised as law enforcement. He certainly was not a religious terrorist killing unarmed citizens. He may have had some combat related mental challenges that caused him to confront a well trained and equipped police force to expose that their show of force is just a show for the cameras and people who want to feel safe. What is the difference between terrorists with bombs and police with bombs? Now this police chief is the new police chief in Chicago, without a winning season in Dallas. But he does have experience with Chicago style law enforcement methods.

And it happened again, just a few days after the Dallas confrontation another disenchanted veteran in Baton Rouge, shot six well-trained uniformed police officers, killing three and wounding three others. The government, police, and the media called this an unprovoked ambush attack on the police. It was like one of those, No-knock warrants raids. It may be too early in this current atmosphere of fear and terror in America to call these two veterans, martyrs. From the information provided to the public, these veterans are no more "terrorists" than rouge police officers, considering they specifically targeted uniformed combatants. This is not a call for or in support of anyone attacking, hurting, or killing anyone for any reason. However, injustice must be addressed and confronted. Sometimes the consequences have been deadly. So now after any mass murder incident involving a veteran as the perpetrator, politicians and the media push the notion that all veterans, especially combat veterans, are suffering from mental disorders and veterans' access to firearms should be closely monitored or restricted.

Another mass shooting, this time in our nation's capital at a military base on minimum security alert status even though our nation is still involved in foreign wars and threatening war at any time! The corporate controlled media and government are spinning a picture that the perpetrator had behavior and religious belief issues that apparently everyone was aware of and did nothing to address their observations or concerns. We're living in a tolerant intolerant period in our unending history. Wouldn't it seem reasonable that if our soldiers had been allowed to at least carry unloaded weapons this incidence may have resulted in fewer unarmed casualties on a military base? After all, we do have the best trained, fed, and tested military on earth. The government claims that we're at war with a diabolically evil insurgent enemy capable of striking anywhere without notice. So, why are our military service members unarmed on our bases or on our street? They are armed on the streets of other countries, and we expect our service members to serve with honor and take responsibility for their actions. There are countless reports of our military personnel being raped, robbed, and murdered on American bases and on American streets. Why not consider having our service members prepared for chaos while we're at war with this formidable invisible adversary walking among us?

Another domestic terrorist attack, this time at a community center in California's gun free zone and our government representatives didn't immediately know what to call it. No surprise to anyone. It took the mayor of Chicago a year to call the killing of an unarmed citizen, a murder by a police officer even when the entire incident was captured on police video. Maybe the science used by some of our elected officials is flawed, misinterpreted or manipulated to imply that somehow more restrictions on citizens and more law enforcement officers are going to stop armed willing individuals from victimizing unarmed defenseless people.

A man walked into a church and killed nine people. He confessed to his victims that he was killing them because of their race. Celebrities make comparisons between the United States which is compiled of fifty independent countries with their own laws pretending to be one country, to little European countries that don't have our population size, cultural diversity, or racist history. No, those countries don't report mass shooting as often as us, but they have mass murders and government-controlled press. They continue to have and support wars of genocide against unarmed defenseless populations. The truth is available for everyone to see. It's on social media, the Internet, and you've seen it with your own eyes. Ask yourself why all of the new gun laws are about protecting the police? Law enforcement and private security experts agree that they are not capable of protecting you from crime.

In Canada, terrorist dressed like soldiers, attacked and killed uniformed police officers in broad daylight, exposing the lie that their police are capable of protecting anyone. It was reported that the police are using all of their resources to understand what happened. The Canadian government's response was to ban and severely restrict civilian firearm ownership. If there's a war taking place on the streets of America, shouldn't all American citizens be prepared to protect themselves? But what's truly festinating is that after each of these mass shooting/mass murders the public is told that everyone knew the perpetrator, knew these people were capable of committing these atrocities and didn't tell anyone or try to intervene for everyone's safety.

Challenge Thirteen

Niggas Ltd. is proud to introduce a new concept in clothing manufacturing. Mulatto brand camouflage clothing and apparel specifically designed to help conceal your Niggas. Mulatto brand will employ state of the art design and manufacturing methods including 3D body scan modeling to insure total concealment of your Niggas. Our environmentally compatible manufacturing techniques will be designed to reduce contamination of our fragile ecosystem. Only organic plant based sustainable/renewable/recyclable fabrics and recyclable synthetic materials will be incorporated into all Mulatto products. Mulatto brand apparel will be manufactured in local facilities, owned and operated by people living in the same community as the workplace. Mulatto will keep you in stylish apparel to meet your concealment requirements.

To address the issue of unemployment in predominately low-income communities, Niggas Ltd., Mulatto brand camouflage clothing will be manufactured in underutilized inner-city locations, converting blight into business for people with the greatest need. Mulatto brand will provide employment opportunities, skills, training, and economic growth, by manufacturing a sustainable product using sustainable materials and fabricating techniques. Not only will artisans, journeymen, designers, business and financial professionals have an opportunity to be innovative, local talented members of the facility's local community will be personally invested in the success of Mulattos. Eminent domain and homesteading laws will be used to make underutilized or abandoned properties available to develop local cottage industries that will be the backbone of American prosperity in the near future.

Niggas Ltd. Mulatto brand camouflage apparel will allow you to blend in no matter where you take your Nigga. Mulatto camouflage apparel is designed to conceal your Bitch in clothing that looks normal and natural in any setting or situation. Mulatto brand camouflage apparel built in holsters and pockets will keep your Nigga in its place and out of sight. Convenient zippered closures allow easy access to your Bitch whenever the need arises. Going to a party? Take your Nigga with you. With Mulatto brand camouflage apparel, no one will ever suspect that your Bitch is within reach. Even Bastards are easy to conceal in Mulatto camouflage. Mulatto camouflage apparel will also keep your Hoes or your Shit out of sight until you want to get your Bitch loaded. Hide your Nigga with Mulatto camouflage apparel and fit right in no matter where you go. Do you have something to hide?

Police Shootings and Misconduct

The police are the front line of government control of African Americans. African Americans cannot blindly trust law enforcement agencies under any circumstance. The police can turn from protector to predator, enforcer to executioner without notice. This year already the number of law enforcement officers involved deaths of US citizens is equal to the number of gangland homicides. Police officers are executing too many US citizens for anyone to feel safe around any of them.

Another officer involved shooting occurred when the California Highway Patrol, entered into a high-speed chase of a suspected stolen vehicle, resulting in the driver of the vehicle being shot and killed, no weapons recovered. Let's also add that the property suspected of being stolen was required by state law to be insured by the owner. In the process of pursuing this suspect in a high-speed chase, several other vehicles were damaged. All of these vehicles are required to be insured. Question: What vested interest do the police have in your property that would be worth taking someone's life for, if you can't take a life for the same reason? Question: Can you go outside, pursue, and kill someone you don't know, just because you believe they may have stolen something from someone you don't know?

Remember, well trained police officers shot and killed an unarmed woman with a child in the backseat of her car, after her rental car crashed into the security barrier at a residential property owned by all Americans (The White House). The officers claim that they had to stop her from continuing to use her car as a terrorist weapon. They say she used her car to ram the fence, and they feared for their safety and yours. They said there could have been a bomb in the car. So, instead of trying to disable the vehicle, they shot into the car to kill the suspect, regardless of the possibility of a bomb or the child's safety. And these are the people who don't want you to have a gun because someone could be killed.

A well-trained Northern California police officer shot and killed a boy for carrying an air rifle in public. The well-trained police officer shot the boy seven times, killing him on the spot because the boy failed to follow police instructions. The police officer must have felt disrespected, disobeyed, and threatened when the boy failed to recognize the plain clothes individual's authority over law abiding citizens minding their own business. This, well-trained police officer shot and killed this boy carrying a toy because this officer, who left the safety of his vehicle and partner to confront a boy, feared for his life. This well-trained, police officer without a report of any shots being fired or threats against the public, exited his vehicle and shot this boy, killing him on the spot because the boy had a toy gun. The police officer said it looked like a real gun to him. He said he felt the public and his life was in danger. It must have been some kind of PTSD that caused this well-trained officer to charge into what he considered a dangerous situation without regard for his own safety. He shot this boy seven times at close range with a .40 caliber semi-automatic pistol in a less than ten second encounter. The officer had a car, a partner, a radio, a Taser, a baton, body armor, and real guns. This well-trained, police officer shot and killed this boy carrying a toy because this officer who left the safety of his vehicle and partner to confront a boy, feared for his life and the public. The officer had a bullet proof vest and a real gun. The boy had a T-shirt and a toy. You don't have to do anything but try to live as a free citizen for the police to feel threatened enough to use deadly force against you. Ask Andy Lopez.

There were several memorial services for the boy, shot and kill for carrying a toy gun in public. There should have been an outcry by everyone, regardless of who or what you are, to bring your toy guns and your children to demonstrate that we will not give up toys so deadly that they can cause well trained police officers to use deadly force against anyone possessing one, including our children! A citizen carrying a toy, or a real firearm should not be a crime unless you are committing a crime with it. Your neighbor being afraid of something is not the same as you threatening your neighbor with something. We should send a message to the government that we will not give up our toys, no matter how many of us they have to kill. I know that I don't feel safe being protected by such well-trained law enforcement officers.

In Florida, a retired police officer with an officially authorized concealed handgun shot and killed a man inside of a movie theater in a dispute over the use of a mobile devise during a movie. Two unarmed movie goers took the gun from the retired police officer without further incidence. More than a hundred-armed uniformed officers in full combat gear arrived on the scene with nothing to do but be a show of force for the TV cameras. Even after surrendering the weapon as a sign of cooperation, the police rush in looking like military commandos with automatic weapons at the ready to control someone who is obviously seeking assistance. They group force the suspects onto the ground to humiliate them with positions of helplessness to restrain a cooperating individual as a show of law enforcement preparedness to control people.

Private security personnel involved in fatal shootings of suspects cite the same rational as the police when they shoot someone: I felt my life was endangered. How does an armed pursuit of an individual put police or private security personnel at risk? What about you, when you're being accosted by criminals or undercover police officers? Shouldn't you have the right to defend yourself? What makes your life less valuable than theirs?

The police officer on transit duty who shot and killed a New Year's Eve celebrator in Oakland, was well-trained, but the court was convinced that the officer unintentionally deployed the wrong weapon that resulted in the death of this unarmed and immobilized US citizen caught in the act of being free. So exactly whose guns need controlling in America? Ask Oscar Grant

San Francisco Bay Areas law enforcement officers are involved in weapons drawn incidences and shootings almost daily. A well-trained police officer assigned to Bay Area Rapid Transit (BART) system shot and killed his partner in the line of duty. With guns drawn they enter the unlocked front door of the unoccupied home of a probation violation suspect. The police were aware the house was unoccupied prior to entering the private home. It was widely reported that during the search, one well trained officer shot the other well-trained officer through the ballistic body armor vest resulting in the officer's death. If the vest had a catastrophic failure, why wasn't there a body armor recall and an investigation of its inability to protect the wearer from common service weapon rounds? The shooting is being called an accident by the police and the corporate media without any common details such as what part of the body was hit allegedly by the single bullet fired. Was he shot in the front, back or side of the vest? Why was the well-trained officer's finger in the trigger housing if no target was identified? The corporate news media flooded their outlets with misinformation and an outpouring of condolences for both officers' families. This police officer on transit system duty shot and killed his partner during a "routine" probation home search.

Today, a well-trained police officer shot and killed a veteran suffering from and struggling with PTSD. They say that the man was determined to be killed by the police. The police

officer was on the scene to prevent the man from killing himself.
Mission accomplished.

Well-trained police officers in Pleasanton, California, shot and
killed a 52-year-old woman because she threatened them with a
fake (replica) handgun. Now they're afraid that her incarcerated
son will seek revenge for her murder.

A well-trained police officer was shot during an altercation with
a US citizen that ensued during what the police describe as a
routine traffic stop. The police, through the corporate media
have painted a picture of the police officer as a victim without
considering that maybe the citizen feared for his life while
being confronted by an armed and threatening person. SFPD
has revised their report to indication that during the traffic
stop which resulted in the officer being shot to say that while
firing at the suspect's car the officer may have been shot by his
partner. I guess it is not as simple as I think. The bullet must
have made an entrance or exit wound? The police have used this
model to prosecute citizens forever. If the bullet was recovered, a
ballistic examination could identify the weapon the round was
fired from, but in San Francisco officials can't determine if one
officer shot another.

Don't assume that when you hear news reports about an officer
involved shooting that the officer was in the right. Everyone has
the right to defend themselves, even from the police. We've seen on
TV, on the news, and with our own eyes what the police will do
to people. How can they have the right to use deadly force when
they feel their lives are in danger, but you don't have the same right
under the same circumstances? Well-trained police officers shoot
and kill Americans every day because the officer believed that
deadly force was the only option to save their own life.

No individual is capable of surviving a shootout with the police. There is no evidence of it, but yes, one or two well-trained police officers could have their hands full with an armed well-trained individual protecting their right to life. Think about the number of deadly firearm incidents the police have exposed, the public too in your lifetime. The police are shooting unarmed men, women, children, and each other in this continuation of the civil war taking place nationwide.

August 2014 a police officer shot and killed an unarmed citizen. More police arrived within minutes creating an overwhelming show of force. Video of this army of police officers closely resembled military special assault units, complete with uniforms, weapons, and vehicles prepared to confront the non-existent enemy combatant. The police on scene immediately formed a defensive offensive posture to protect themselves as if the officer who did the shooting was the slain victim and the public was the enemy. Demonstrations and civil unrest followed. More military style police officers arrived employing those military tactics, weapons, and vehicles, as if they were confronting foreign invaders. America has a history and culture of blaming and attacking victims. The world sees the US collapsing on itself through an escalation of laws that are contrary to the long held American principal that no one is above the law.

There is no reason that a suspect should be shot with more than forty rounds from a variety of police weapons. This kind of excessive use of force cannot be justified as safe for the public unless you believe that police bullets are less deadly, with less chance of stray bullets hitting civilians than bullets fired by criminals during drive by shootings. The police cannot be allowed to shoot or kill people for things that you can't use deadly force against someone for. Judgement and execution are the court's responsibility.

A well-trained police officer shot and killed an American for pointing an electronic Taser, at the officer during the altercation. Was the citizen acting in self-defense or was the police officer? We'll never know. If you find yourself in this situation, the police and our current laws require you to surrender. In Santa Clara County, California, two well-trained police officers shot and killed a woman who was wielding a knife. The woman failed to follow their orders to immediately put the knife down. I guess she must have been like the warrior princess. Both officers had Tasers, mace, and batons, but chose to use deadly force against the woman. The woman's family had called 911 because she was off her meds and behaving strangely. The police responded.

This week there was another incident of a police officer shooting and killing an unarmed citizen. The citizen was an accident injury victim seeking emergency assistance at a stranger's house. The frightened occupants of the house called the police to report a prowler on their property. On arrival the police immediately opened fire shooting the injured accident victim ten times. The police were allegedly responding to a report of attempted home invasion. These are split second life and death decisions.

Two more murders in Minnesota and Louisiana by Police officers were captured on cell phone video and streamed live over social media. In the Minnesota incident the victim's girlfriend and their child were in the vehicle when the execution took place. She can be heard pleading for her life while the police officer killed this American in front of a child. The victim's crime was being a passenger in a vehicle with a broken taillight. Now that's some serious motor vehicle law enforcement! The victim attempting to comply with the officer's instructions identified himself as a licensed firearm owner prior to being shot. The police have demonstrated time and again that even armed citizens are no match for our nation's finest law enforcement officers and agencies.

A group of plain clothes and uniform NYPD officers physically attacked and choked a man to death. The police were not a witness to any alleged illegal activity by the man. But because the police were such heavily armed authorities, the unarmed helpless witnesses were afraid to intervene. The incident was captured on cell phone video. There were approximately twenty officers involved, and they did nothing to stop this brutal attack on a citizen begging for his life. He was suspected of selling individual cigarettes to people willing to buy them. Was this a civil infraction warranting a death sentence? Just think, even with the multitude of apparent physical, social and personal challenges this individual may have been exhibiting, he may have made it home alive if not for this brief encounter with dedicated law enforcement.

Most of the court ordered ballistic forensic tests for bullets collected at a crime scene where the police exchanged gun fire with suspects are for bullets fired by law enforcement officers. Imagine how many bullets that can be. Imagine how much it cost to determine that police bullets went everywhere. Most missing their intended targets causing property damage, accidental injury and death.

To keep you safe, the police use secret interrogation facilities, new high-performance cars, expensive to maintain military vehicles, aircraft, equipment, and weapons, high-capacity ammunition magazines, body cameras, and re-training. These things cost a lot of money, and you don't feel safe.

African Americans don't need police with body cameras to see abuses by the police. Americans have been watching this stuff in movies since motion pictures were invented. We the decedents of American slaves and enslavers have been telling the world this ever since we arrived here. Imagine living in a country where you have never felt safe and it's your country. Ask the people of South Africa.

Challenge Fourteen

Nigga Ltd. in response to the murder of an unarmed and underage citizen by well-trained law enforcement officers and the recommendations by our elected officials that toy guns to be made from clear or brightly colored materials as a way to keep police officers safe, Niggas Ltd. is introducing: The Devil. The Devil is our next generation, three shot, semi-automatic pistol. Unlike our redeemer pistol, the Lord, a fourth round can be loaded before the three round magazine is fitted to the weapon. It is designed to resemble a toy pistol constructed entirely of advanced composite and ceramic materials. The Devil will be available in .44 magnum and .50 calibers in a variety of clear and bright florescent colors.

The Devil is the perfect companion for people who live in areas where the police are trained to treat all brightly colored weapons as toys. The Devil can be open carried without a permit because the police will not be able to distinguish it from a child's plaything. But the Devil is a deceiver delivering a lethal dose of hell and damnation to anyone who underestimates what it can do for you. Non-believers will be quickly converted when they encounter the Devil.

Using 3-D and AI manufacturing technology the Devil will have no external moving parts making it even more indistinguishable from toys. It will utilize the same electronic user recognition technology as our other limited capacity semi-automatic pistol, the Lord. This technology will leave a permanent mark of the beast on anyone other than the registered owner firing the weapon.

To the police and perpetrators, the Devil will appear as a harmless brightly colored or clear toy. It will be capable of deceiving even the most well-trained law enforcement officer and learned politicians. The Devil may not save your life in a gunfight with an army of law enforcement officers or wanton criminals, but the Devil is deadly when it's just you and a perpetrator who doesn't believe the Devil is real. Remember the Devil is not to be played with. It is not a toy, but get the Devil loaded with some of our biggest Ho's and let the soul searching begin. It is a lethal deceiver designed to send anyone wishing to do you harm straight to hell.

Take responsibility

The police shoot people every day if you see our country as nightly news reports. I see America as it is, fifty individual countries in a tenuous alliance pretending to be one country. Shootings by criminals, police or anyone else may be a rare occurrence where you live. But across the nation police are responsible for killing far too many people for us to trust any of them exclusively with our safety or protection. Excessive force and intimidation are a common tactic employed by police to keep citizens under control. Most people cooperate and surrender to police authority to avoid forceful encounters with them. Rarely does the court determine police wrongdoing even when there is video eyewitness evidence of police misconduct. State law authorizes the use of deadly force when officers feel their lives are endangered. What is your right? It can't just be surrender when split second life and death decisions are be made involving you. Police always claim they fear for their lives after shooting anyone. If the average person is a potential deadly threat to armed uniformed police officers, who should we the people be afraid of? Police officers say that they issued instructions to all of the unarmed victims prior to killing them in self-defense. I can't believe that these free Americans didn't immediately comply with instructions from their masters. Could you imagine slapping your twelve-year-old child in the face at home or in public because they didn't immediately follow your instructions? Could you imagine a teacher slapping your child because they didn't immediately comply with the teacher's instructions? How can it ever be acceptable? But a police officer in uniform or undercover can shoot and kill your child in a ten second encounter because your child did not immediately follow the instructions of a stranger yelling at them from a moving vehicle. Could it be that maybe these attacks by police on citizens are mostly about privilege, ego, respect, power and immunity? Question: What is the difference between a police officer killing your child in a ten second encounter from a moving vehicle and a drive by shooting? Official answer: The police officer's life was in danger.

There are laws prohibiting citizens impersonating police officers, but the police can dress up and impersonate the people we're told to be afraid of. We're all familiar with reports of police officers impersonating prostitute street walkers resulting in massive arrests, property seizers, and lucrative fines that benefit police departments. Undercover officers have a well-documented history of impersonating criminals, dressing like criminals, driving criminal's cars, participating in criminal activities and mob actions in the name of fighting crime. Police departments have been enriching themselves with the spoils of war in the process. I wonder how many drive-by shootings have police officers been a ride-along on? We are not supposed to be afraid of the police.

Not all police homicides are justified or necessary. The police are not always right, impartial, or innocent. The police are not supposed to be the judge, jury, and executioner of Americans. The police have cost the American people billions in wrongful death law suites and continue to take Americans lives. The police should have no special powers over Americans and no special protection from prosecution in court. The local police are not officers of the court, but recipients of the public trust. A trust they have broken continuously. The US Justice Department has recently released reports regarding a culture of excessive force by law enforcement officers and agencies against citizens nationwide.

When the police come to a peaceful demonstration armed and prepared for confrontation, couldn't that be construed as provocation for confrontation? If the police, known to use deadly force against unarmed civilians, come to peaceful demonstrations armed, should anyone feel safe? What if law enforcement officers participated in peaceful demonstrations for police reforms as unarmed, ununiformed, marchers in the demonstrations? Without the guns and colors (uniforms), police would look just like everyone else participating in the event. Then they would be culpable with and venerable to whatever happens. They could also inconspicuously discourage or encourage crimes against property and disruption of public safety. Like those police officers in New York, riding with a group of motorcyclists that participated in a terror attack on a frightened family and motoring public trapped in their cars on a busy roadway when the motorcyclists decided to block all lanes of traffic. The officers were armed and although no one was killed during the assault, those officers failed to stop the attack or protect the family or the public.

At the graduation ceremony for the New York City Police Academy, on duty police officials and sworn officers of the law turned their backs to the mayor in a demonstration of their disdain for the citizens they're paid to serve. No respect for the office of the mayor, no respect for the public. All of the NYPD commanders should have been disciplined and the rest of the force should have been required to walk a beat and use public transportation to remind them to respect the public they're paid to serve. Police officers are not overseers of the people, they operate under the auspices and will of the citizens.

Challenge Fifteen

Niggas Ltd. would like to invite all Americans to participate in the introduction, marketing, and use of House Niggas. House Niggas are a virtual and human involvement security system that incorporates immersion technology, highly educated individuals, and former military personnel. House Niggas will be the very first, independent contractor, voluntary free indentured service exchange in America since the Emancipation Proclamation.

The government and the media continue to remind us that the world is dangerous. They both encourage us to rely on technologies that are impossible to secure. The government can't protect itself from cyber security failures. Do you really want to trust your family and home's security to internet connections, cell phone Wi-Fi and cloud data storage? House Niggas security systems are custom designed to provide you with a level of security that was previously the exclusive privilege of the wealthy. Depending on the client's needs, House Niggas can provide you with as few as one live-in college graduate, former military member, or as many House Niggas as necessary to meet your security requirements.

These are real people working with real people for personal security protection. According to law enforcement agencies the presence of people is one of the best deterrents to home invasion and physical attacks on the street. House Niggas are available for in-home security and as mobile companions. All potential clients and House Niggas are screened and interviewed for compatibility and safety.

House Niggas is a full-service security provider with no out of pocket expense to the client. You decide the level of security you need and let Niggas Ltd. provide you with House Niggas to serve you with our no cost for security personnel service. House Niggas is an on-site live-in security service with technology assisted security surveillance. House Niggas live with you, travel with you and monitor your security surveillance equipment to help keep you and your family safe. Niggas Ltd. can provide you with armed and unarmed House Niggas to protect you or your property for free. House Niggas and clients are required to sign a "No Cost Living Space" agreement and a "No Pay Security Service" contract. House Niggas are bonded to assure clients receive services superior to all others.

House Niggas are educated, disciplined, and trustworthy independent contractors who specialize in providing a human element of security for you, your family, or your home in exchange for a place to live. Having House Niggas living in your home or on your property provides you with an unparalleled element of personal security. By taking in House Niggas, you will be contributing to the success of exceptional individuals who just need an affordable place to live. House Niggas willingly accept the tremendous responsibility of caring for and protecting others as an intricate aspect of your personal security requirements. House Niggas are free (No Pay for Service). Clients provide acceptable living space and conditions in exchange for human security support as agreed by jointly signed contract. House Niggas and client relationships can be mutually emancipated per written proclamation at any time. Because House Niggas are independent contractors and not tenants, landlord-tenant laws may not apply.

You can have as few as one House Nigga as a house sitter for the summer or an entire family style security unit with specially trained children to escort and attend school with your children. You decide on the number and kinds of House Niggas you can use. Because House Niggas provide security services for free, clients may want to employ them to perform a variety of non-security related services such as housekeeping, cooking, driving, and gardening for an agreed benefit. Note: Niggas Ltd. only provides House Niggas for security services. All other agreements are strictly between individual House Niggas and clients.

House Niggas will serve you and your family for free. House Niggas provides you with peace of mind that the government and corporations are not controlling the security of your family and property. All House Niggas are bonded after completing 40 hours of training at the Plantation. Take a House Niggas with you as personal bodyguards or leave House Niggas at home to protect your family and property. They live with you, and we here at Niggas Ltd. believe House Niggas are like family you can fire. So, go ahead, leave home on business or vacation and trust House Niggas to take care of your spouse, children, and property for free. You can trust House Niggas from Niggas Ltd.

Private Security

Everywhere you look there are new armed private security operations and services. Communities around the country are now hiring private armed security forces to supplement public police services. These are armed individuals, many without official police training or authority, in uniforms that resemble police carrying firearms in the open in strict gun control states like California and Illinois exercising police powers. These are the armed individuals with military style weapons and equipment we encounter at night clubs, sporting events, outdoor concerts, banks, coffee shops, grocery stores, liquor stores, cannabis dispensaries, retail stores, manufacturing facilities and patrolling neighborhoods under the color of law. Private armed security services driving around neighborhoods in vehicles marked with the word "Police" on the car and their uniforms. Many large corporations have their own police department with state sanctioned power to detain citizens and issue citations with fees attached and enforced by local courts. And let's not forget the celebrities, politicians, wealthy individuals and privileged people who have plain clothes armed private bodyguards and security patrols for their personal protection while trying to convince you to exclusively depend on government provided protection. Thousands of Americans have been violated, abused and murdered during encounters with private security.

When it comes to persuading police officers to abandon public service nothing tops the lucrative salaries offered by armed private security companies. Much like the military losing many specially trained troops to mercenary like companies such as Academi (aka Blackwater), police departments can't compete with the benefits offered by private security companies.

Private securities agencies are granted many of the same authorities as the public law enforcement officers including the use of deadly force. All of these armed entities are under someone's control, not yours. No law enforcement agency or elected public official is demanding the prohibition of firearms for private security organizations because so many off-duty police officers, former officers, and military veterans are employed by these companies.

All of the armed private security personnel you see every day are just people with guns. How is it possible for these agencies to employ off duty police officers when police are never considered to be "off duty", according to police unions? Isn't this why they're authorized to be armed at all times? Elected officials, corporate executives and media celebrities also employ private security agents as armed bodyguards and home security. They too are just people with guns. But corporate media, government agencies and celebrities have not addressed this as a public safety issue.

Now thousands of civilian para-military groups disguised as police have assumed autonomy of life and death of US citizens when they believe their lives are endangered. African Americans have been subjected to murderous abuse by criminals and law enforcement officers since we arrived in this country. Trust history.

Challenge Sixteen

In response to the increased use of drone technology by law enforcement agencies, major corporations, and private citizens, Niggas Ltd. is introducing our first defender drone. The Spear Chucker is a stealth drone using technologically advanced composite materials, solar power, high dynamic range cameras, and powerful lasers to detect and disable unauthorized commercial drone intrusion. The Spear Chucker is completely undetectable by unauthorized drones and will employ electronic interruption technology and physical intervention to disable unauthorized drones. The Spear Chucker will be held on your property by a technologically advanced chain to prevent the Spear Chucker from escaping your control and to provide direct power and data transfer. The Spear Chucker can be deployed in fully autonomous, manual and programed modes.

Law enforcement agencies, corporations, hobbyists, and criminals are increasing their intrusion into our lives using drone technology to monitor your private activities. The data collected by the predatory use of drones is being used not only to watch criminal activity and for commercial marketing, but to monitor your movement and property. Law enforcement and criminals share this information to exploit your vulnerabilities.

With a Spear Chucker drone chained to your property you'll never have to worry about unauthorized intrusion or surveillance of your private activities at home. All captured predatory drones, their components, cargo and attachments, can be confiscated for use as evidence of intrusion. Spear Chucker drones can be paired with your neighbors Spear Chucker to provide protection for everyone.

Call to Action

This is the African American veteran's experience. Every military conflict the United States have been involved in, our government has armed African Americans to defend this country's interest while our fundamental rights as full citizens have been denied by federal, state and local laws and practice. As soon as African Americans return from the fight, the law is changed to disarm us, leaving us defenseless to all domestic threats, mistreatment, and terror. After each war, just when our communities are beginning to reap the benefit of fighting for this country, the unwanted people (poor, uneducated, unemployable, mentally ill, immigrants, criminals and police) are systematically channeled into our communities. This increases crime and police presence contributing to the destabilization of economic growth and feelings of despair among the people. It is not these people's fault, even though we do contribute to the issue. It's not the fault of the police either, because they have issues trying to control free people. Guns are not the answer to our problems, but your right to defend yourself is human and the right to be armed is American.

All Veterans, we took a blood oath to protect and defend the Constitution and the People of the United States of America.

That oath did not end with your honorable separation from service. So why are veterans being required to request permission from any law enforcement agency to exercise a right we earned by blood? Disarmed veterans anywhere on earth are known as Prisoners of War.

All military veterans should arm themselves as an act of civil disobedience, national security and patriotism. Having said that, please don't take this as a call for you to dress up like soldiers or quasi-paramilitary militia patriots displaying your weapons for the cameras. If I see someone walking down the street with an uncased or un-holstered weapon, don't blame me for feeling unsafe and taking a defensive position. Please don't do this. People are already afraid. If you are going to participate, please get some firearm safety training. Make sure that the weapon is in your legal possession. Be prepared to lose your freedom, your weapon and your right to be armed, be required to pay a fine, be labeled a convicted felon and lose your right to vote. Veterans should go about their daily routine as much as possible avoiding unnecessary exposure of and attention to their firearms. Understand that you could be killed by a police officer for their safety if they even see what they perceive to be a weapon on your person or within reach. Veterans, I know that some of us are going to become prisoners and casualties of this action. Many will be arrested, physically injured and killed. This is already happening, and you were not looking for a fight. This is not about a mass gathering of people where things can go out of order. This must be an individual act of collective civil disobedience orchestrated to commence on a given date. This is how easy it is to turn law-abiding citizens into criminals. Ask Martin Luther King, Jr.

If there is a war on the streets of America perpetrated by terrorists, gangs and murders shouldn't veterans be excluded from firearm possession restrictions nationwide? This assault on US citizens by law enforcement has been escalated from simple financial extortion though through traffic violations to real property seizer and civil forfeiture to fund an insurgent army disguised as police with the power to accost, detain, abuse, and execute citizens without trials or convictions. Our country has always been this way for African Americans.

Attention: All military veterans, active duty and reserve service member, especially African American veterans with proof of honorable discharge. Go to your US Congressional Representative's or Senator's office and demand that your state issue a CCW to you on demand. It sounds crazy but you will be asking them to give you something that is already yours.

We have already demonstrated our patriotic defense of the Constitution through personal sacrifice to our country. This alone should entitle us to any means of self-defense equal to your local police. It is your sworn duty to defend this country from all enemies, foreign and domestic. You in fact pledged your life to it. You gave a blood oath, and many have paid far beyond the metals, hospitals, and loans. Yet, you are being forced by a heavily armed entity other than the US military to be an unarmed victim of an uncivil war being waged on the streets where you live.

The government has admitted that it has lost control of everyone's personal data and secret information in its care to a cyber terrorist attack. Criminals and governments are both preying on defenseless citizens for resources. Each state has its own armed forces, the National Guard. Some governors and media personalities want you to believe that the National Guard is our professional well-trained government-controlled militia. However, the constitution does not recognize any National Guard as militia. Understand that some National Guard members may also be members of religious organizations, street gangs, motorcycle gangs, terrorist organizations, private militia groups, private security companies, or law enforcement agencies. They may even be your relative or neighbor. Your right to be armed is not constitutionally dependent on your participation in a militia to exercise your right to be armed for personal protection.

Veterans should follow Martin Luther King Jr's instruction to fill up the jails through acts of civil disobedience to laws that deny humane opportunities to everyone. Look around where you live. Do the police have new cars? Where do you think they got the money?

All US citizens should defy these gun control laws, especially African American veterans. Self-defense is everyone's natural right. When law enforcement can't distinguish law-abiding citizens from criminals, and citizens can't distinguish police from criminals, all citizens should be armed if they choose for personal safety. People continue to lose their livelihood, property and die as a result of the government and law enforcement agencies continuing to practice something that has never worked. When what you're doing has never worked, it's time to try something new. Ask Barrack Obama.

The President was correct when he said we must do something about the gun rights issue. I propose that all military veterans be exempt from all firearm laws related to possession and concealment immediately. A veteran should only have to show their honorable separation from service identification card to authorities when requested and not have to surrender their weapons except in the commission of a crime. This should apply in all 50 states immediately. This action will make it safer for veterans travelling around the country they swore with their lives to protect. Too many veterans have lost their lives and livelihoods just for possessing a tool that no police officer or criminal would leave home without. The President should go to the congress with an executive order to wave all firearm possession restrictions on veterans nationwide. If America is already in a ground war on American soil, why wouldn't we want our veterans who have sworn an oath with their lives to be active allies to society and not continue to make them handicapped victims of crime?

There are unknown numbers of warring factions operating all over the US. Some of them wear law enforcement uniforms. All of them wear symbols to clearly identify them as having control over some territory and all are members of families and clans, and they are heavily armed according to the police. Veterans, it is our right to protect ourselves, families, and property at all times no matter where you are in this country or who you have to protect yourselves from. America has never been safe for African Americans, but especially our veterans.

I'm not suggesting that every African American run out and make firearm manufactures wealthier than they are already. This is a call for African Americans to begin manufacturing firearms in our own facilities to enrich our communities and provide for our country's security. The largest firearm manufactures advertise their products in the most racist pro-gun publications available, and none of these firearm or publishing companies are owned by African Americans.

We need to discuss the idea that African Americans could form collectives across the country to homestead abandoned properties in blighted areas of our cities. To develop, own, and operate firearms training facilities. Military surplus simulators, no live fire weapons or bullets could be used to provide firearm safety training and marksmanship for sport, recreation, and self-defense to the general public. The more access to education you can have, the better it is for everyone. According to the government, firearm safety training is essential to reducing firearm accidents and deaths. African American veterans could perform every aspect of the operation including homesteading and rehabilitating the properties, installing, operating, and maintaining the simulators, weapons, and facilities. Many vets are jobless, homeless, emancipated from the incarceration, educated, employed, entrepreneurs, and retired. All vets have useful skills which should be utilized to create communities. Collectively, we could demand that the government invest in this kind of facility to provide jobs in communities suffering from economic despair. It would also provide a much need service for communities suffering from crime and violence. For African Americans, it would be an opportunity to own and operate businesses where permanent employment opportunities are needed most.

It will not be easy. There will be resistance and competition once we begin to seek public support, available resources, and private financial assistance. We will have to invest ourselves in making it happen. Some of you are already thinking about why this can't work instead of how to make it happen. I can't help you with how not to do something. But if we are tired of being victims of complacency, excuses, handouts and controls that only hold us down, this is just one idea to change this condition and mentality.

Heroes

I see so many older veterans running marathons and corporations, yet the government is afraid to allow these well-trained "Heroes" the right they've earned through personal sacrifice to their country. We honor their sacrifice by forcing them to be victims of violence and intimidation by criminals and police in the name of public safety. There have been brazen lethal attacks on our military service members here at home. Many of our elected representatives believe that restricting active military members and veteran's right to self-defense has had a positive impact on crime. They must think that more crime is better. There are millions of unarmed active-duty service members, veterans, and their families living outside the safety of our bases. Our elected officials have insane justifications for military bases being safer with unarmed soldiers, guarded by armed civilian contractors and local law enforcement. Our service members are at risk, venerable to criminal terror attacks every day travelling between work and home. Our military is all volunteer citizens sworn to defend us from all enemies and trained to use the weapons issued to them. Veterans, our national heroes, shouldn't be prohibited from carrying for lawful purposes common weapons anywhere law enforcement officers are not restricted. If the State of (your State here) is determined to be the leader in gun control regulation, it should immediately upon request, issue concealed carry permits to all honorably discharged military veterans and encourage all other states to do the same. Military veterans, "America's Heroes", our champion defenders of freedom have already been trained in safety and proper use of firearms.

It seems unfair and almost immoral to ask our citizens to put their lives on the line to defend the lives and rights of people around the world, but consider veterans incapable or incompetent to defend themselves, their families, or their property at home. Veterans have already given their full measure of devotion and deserve every right in the constitution. Veterans should not be forced to become victims of crime across America. The license or permit issued to veterans should be valid in all states because when we swore to defend this country, it is for the entire country and not just the state we live in. Veterans, concealed carry status could be identified on a driver's license for law enforcement and Veterans' safety.

Veterans currently leaving active military service and retired police officers could be enlisted to conduct any required certification training and the federal government could issue permits or license to veterans that successfully complete the training. This would give law enforcement agencies an opportunity to work directly with the law-abiding public to address the issue of firearm safety and provide another tool in the effort to curb crime in America. Any additional training regarding local laws can be provided at publically owned weapons ranges such as those at police facilities.

My personal safety is my personal responsibility according to the US Supreme Court. A reasonable means to protect myself is written in the Constitution. To assure Americans freedom in America the president should sign an executive order stating that all honorably discharged military service members are entitled to carry legal firearms (open or concealed) for legal purposes without a special license from any state. All that should be required is a DD form 214, Certificate of Release or Discharge from Active Duty. This will cause an immediate drop in the crime rate all over the country. Because being an armed and civil responsible veteran would no longer be a crime. Yes, there will be a short rise in firearm related injury and deaths as criminals and police adjust to the change. All other citizens requesting permission to be armed should have to complete firearm safety situational awareness and personal responsibility training.

Challenge Seventeen

Niggas Ltd., Mulatto brand products is proud to introduce a new concept in personal body armor we call: The LGBTQ (Like Government Ballistic Tactical Quality) personal protection body armor. The LGBTQ body armor is a bullet proof vest to be manufactured using state of the art high strength sustainable ballistic fabric from organic hemp compounds and insect generated fibers. The LGBTQ will have energy absorbing ceramic inserts developed from recyclable silica compounds and fitted into pockets strategically positioned in the vest to protect vital organs and mitigate ballistic impact.

Deadly encounters with criminals and law enforcement are increasing daily. LGBTQ body armor is designed to provide you with the ultimate in personal body protection. You won't have to look like a soldier or police officer either. LGBTQ personal protection body armor will come in a rainbow of finishes to suit your style, individual preference, social identity, for the level of protection desired.

To address the issue of unemployment in disenfranchised communities, Niggas Ltd., Mulatto brand, LGBTQ personal protection body armor will be manufactured in abandoned inner city manufacturing facilities, converting blight into business for people with the greatest need. LGBTQ body armor manufacturing facilities will be owned and operated by people living in the same community as the factory.

When a dangerously queer situation arises, LGBTQ personal protection body armor can save your ass or your life. LGBTQ will keep you stylish and safe while expressing your unique individualism in an ever increasingly hostile and deadly world. LGBTQ is fully compatible with all of our Niggas Ltd, products. Our inclusive community of dedicated scientists, engineers, and skilled craft people have created an effective partner you can come out in when hiding in the closet is not an option.

An Un-Civil War

There is a war on the streets of America. Not just in the big cities, but in every nook and cranny of our nation. Unarmed Americans are the primary victims of this un-civil war. Unarmed Americans caught between armed and organized groups conducting a war over our resources and lives for their benefit. Admit it. We're being duped by the government, law enforcement, and the media regarding our safety. Doesn't it seem like the more we spend on law enforcement the more laws we get and the scarier our country seems? Today we filled up the privately owned prisons for violations of laws we didn't know exist. African Americans fear each other as much as we fear everyone else. African Americans are the largest group of perpetrators and victims of violence and murder nationwide on TV. In real life, law enforcement agencies participate in many of the atrocities perpetrated against African Americans in the name of public safety and we fear the police more than anything else.

A defenseless individual cannot defeat an organized group of armed individuals working as a team or a unit. The problem with policing is assumed authority over the people, the license to kill and exemption from responsibility. We the people are defenseless to oppose them or protect ourselves from them or any other perpetrators. I'm not trying to convince you to arm yourself. I just don't like the idea that an organized group of armed people conducting a war where I live expects me to depend on them for my safety.

The United States has withdrawn our military from two foreign battlefields and brought them home to a dysfunctional government that is only proficient at collecting revenue from its citizens. The state and local governments are no better. The criminal justice system and law enforcement organizations are dependent on the proliferation of crime to justify the extortion of the citizens. And there are so many laws that with today's technology by the time you surrender your license, registration, and insurance papers to law enforcement they know more about you than your family and what they can use to detain you under the color of law. Because driving on public roads is a privilege, your protection from unreasonable search, seizure, and detention are rendered irrelevant by state and local law for public safety. You never know what law you're breaking. Because cause to stop is cause to search. And what do they find? Americans, armed because we're tired of being afraid, robbed, kidnapped, raped, and murdered on the streets, roads, trails, and highways of America.

Our government is openly funding a war on crime, drugs, and guns. It is being waged against US citizens without an official declaration of war. Homeland Security laws are being used as a covert type of martial law against people too frightened to question authority or resist. Under the new homeland security rules, it seems like open season on citizens by law enforcement. There is no reason that law enforcement should cost so much and solve so little with the money and power to stop, search, detain, punish and execute Americans at will.

It is not always a crime to resist the police unless you are breaking the law. Americans are supposed to resist any attack on our inalienable rights. But today the police determine what our rights are. Let's have some new rules of engagement. Can't we agree that the threat of deadly force is not required to issue most traffic citations or talk to people on the street even if that person is armed? You and I encounter armed individuals every day. Most of them are in uniform and many are not. But all of them are armed and the group we call police, have been involved in every kind of crime known to human beings including murder. An armed American should not be an issue to any law enforcement officer unless shots are fired at them. Any law prohibiting armed self-defense is unconstitutional.

Thank you for your service

Every day, members of our well-trained military are being discharged onto the streets of America. I wonder how those service members are going to feel when they discover that because they have been encouraged to be diagnosed and treated for "Post Traumatic Stress Disorder" (a mental condition), that under expanded gun control laws veterans will be prohibited from purchasing, owning, or possessing any firearms, or even being employed! Thanks for your service!

History reminds us that people without the means to support themselves will turn to the government or to crime for assistance, and against each other to get what they need to survive. We could put veterans with challenges to work rebuilding our infrastructure. Oh, I forgot the military reduced its common skills training in favor of highly specialized fighting forces. Instead, we hire private contractors to provide common skills resources to the military and those companies outsource the labor to citizens of poor countries because hiring and training Americans is too expensive. I wonder where the money comes from (taxes, fees, fines, forfeitures, confiscations, leans…).

Just think of all of those firearm range instructors becoming available when they leave the military. They could open rifle and pistol ranges with a focus on urban firearm use and safety for the general public. If we can teach sex and driver education in schools, and if gun safety is really a major concern, then it seems reasonable that teaching firearm safety should be a curriculum.

It is a human right to keep and bear arms for defense. Possession of a firearm cannot be made illegal according to the US Supreme Court. But it has been, especially for African Americans. But there is a much bigger problem. What are we going to do with so many discharged service members without jobs? I wonder how many former specialized forces members will be operating some kind of counter insurgency or Special Weapons and Tactics (SWAT) schools inside the US, training law enforcement agencies, private security and militia groups, military tactics. How many of these schools will be owned and operated by African Americans? Are African Americans even aware that these types of operations and opportunities exist?

After Thoughts

The next time someone ask: Why does anyone need an assault rifle or large capacity magazines? Please ask them to imagine what would happen if you encountered a criminal perpetrator armed with a modern assault style rifle and you only have a mobile phone. I don't know what law enforcement officials are afraid of. They carry fully automatic military grade weapons. This means that they are armed no different than the soldiers and civilians at the time of the American Revolution. But George Washington didn't have helicopters, satellites, drones, cameras, armored vehicles, cell phones, computers or the Internet, or a country consisting of fifty individual country-states with well-established laws and their own armies to defend them. There weren't any cities in America with millions of people living in them either. But there were laws exclusive to Negros everywhere. If you take the concept of race out of the equation, then this story fits every immigrant to ever come to America. But only Negros, were stripped of every recollection of who they were and continuously denied rights for all Americans. We continue to do the same things and expect different results.

I can understand that prior to the civil war and before Brown Vs the Board of Education that maybe some African Americans could read and write in English. Today we graduate from the best universities in America and around the world. So why are we still relying on someone else to interpret the Constitution for us. The people who created this document for the most part did not have an education equivalent to today's high school graduates. But even they could tell you that our current government representatives are not serving the people very well if they don't understand that the right to be armed is essential to freedom. I personally believe that all US citizens in every state, city, town, and village should defy the unconstitutional prohibition against personal protection. No police officer will leave their home without a loaded gun on their person.

In America, We the People, enforce the law. Not the police. The police cannot protect us from the police, not to mention protecting us from crimes being perpetrated against us by each other. The police attitude regarding an assault on your person is based on the level of resources required to protect you. We have been traumatized with a feeling of helplessness that police rarely experience because they carry their courage in a holster and are mostly exempt from responsibility. Your cell phone is gone. The cell phone is easy to replace. But your sense of safety has been irretrievably stolen.

While we are being shown images of terrorist training camps for children in other parts of the world, our children are being murdered in the street by well-trained police officers for possessing toys. I'm not advocating against our necessity for law enforcement. Our children are killing each other and frightening the communities they live in. I am not advocating dismantling law enforcement agencies. But absolute change is required. I'm not advocating indiscriminately arming anyone. I'm advocating a citizen's right to self-defense without interference from the police when no crime is being committed. If you don't feel safe where you live in America, what can you do?

When it comes to taking your money, the government doesn't care about your racial or sexual identity or your political preference. The ability to extract payment from you is all that matters. But too many individual renegade-rouge police officers and many other Americans just don't like black people! And they will kill Negro looking citizens even when they can see that you are not armed and pose no threat to them. Fleeing, escaping, and not immediately following police instruction is not a threat and should be expected from people fearing for their life. I'm not saying or insinuating that all police are corrupt or a danger to society. I'm saying that the police have nothing to fear from armed law-abiding citizens. Just like citizens should have nothing to fear from armed police officers.

Like my brother says, how can there be any good police officers if they are afraid of each other? Police expect you, with no means of self-defense or protection, to give them information about criminal activity where you live. Funny, isn't it? When law abiding citizens are asked to help solve crimes, we freely give this assistance to the government as good citizens do. When we don't, it's because of fear. We have to protect ourselves from criminals, the police, the court, and each other.

Challenge Eighteen

Niggas Ltd. would like to invite you all to participate in the development, marketing, and sales of the Mother Fucker. Mother Fuckers will be available in two sizes: The Big Mother Fucker, 12-inch-long barrel chambered for .50 Cal. and the Little Mother Fucker, 4-inch barrel chambered for .357 magnums. Get your Mother Fucker loaded with a couple of Niggas Ltd. Ho's and you will be ready for whatever comes. All steel, two shot, semi-automatic slide breech gas operated pistol with ambidextrous safety lock, heavy weight, and inexpensive. These Mother Fuckers come in your choice of blue-black, black and blue or bright white stainless-steel barrels and frames with checkered past grips.

All the perpetrator needs to do is see a Mother Fucker to stop them in their tracks. These Mother Fuckers are specifically developed to be impressive and functional. Both are massive tools requiring a firm two hand grip to keep them under control. Mother Fuckers can be used unloaded to beat off an attacker after firing your Ho's and replacing them in the moment is not an option. Its natural point handgrip and hefty steel frame make it a useful bludgeon. Nothing connects with a perpetrator like a Mother Fucker upside their head.

When size and weight are not an issue the Big Mother Fucker is for you. Pull a Big Mother Fucker out of your pants and watch what happens. Twelve inches of cold hard blue-black steel will command the attention of anyone planning to fuck with you. The Little Mother Fucker is thick and heavy. You'll want to hold it just like the Big Mother Fucker. Although it's shorter than its sibling, when you pull a bright Little Mother Fucker out, they'll stop and surrender or get fucked up by a couple of Ho's. Both Mother Fuckers will be affordable, easy to use, and low maintenance. You'll feel safe and protected with either of these Mother Fuckers. If your Mother Fucker is slow to go off, like other Niggas they can be adjusted with a little coin and a screw. No one wants a Mother Fucker in their face, but it's nice to know you have a Big Mother Fucker in your pants. Grab a Mother Fucker with both hands before you shoot. The Little Mother Fucker can be held with one hand, but it is thick and heavy, and it jumps hard when shooting. If you miss your mark, you can shoot again or beat them off with it. Mother Fuckers don't just look dangerous, they are.

Remember

Remember those crazies, criminals, and police are mostly attacking people in places where they know the victims are unarmed and unable to fight back. They're not attacking trained, alert, and armed individuals or places where they congregate like your local shooting range.

With all of the paramilitary private contractors training and working in our country, including on our military/government installations, it won't be long before these places are attacked. Oh, that's right it has already happened. Not at the police departments where everyone is armed, it's happened on our military bases where our soldiers are not.

You can't keep what you can't protect. Buying insurance does not excuse your personal responsibility and your life can't be repaired when you're dead. Law abiding Americans systematically are being denied a basic human right in the name of public safety in an environment that is not safe. The German people watched their guardians exterminate millions of defenseless human beings. First their government introduced government mandated gun registration for public safety. Then they passed laws to criminalize the people and confiscated guns to render them defenseless for public safety. Then they attacked them. There was a lot of money being made by everyone except for those people considered undesirable. Those undesirable people had paid their taxes for protection but were sacrificed for power and control of public safety. Everyone made money and every ally got a little something in return for their participation. Every American who served in uniform during WII became more American except for the undesirable people, like African Americans. After the war we were even more demonized than the enemies of humanity that we fought against for American values. It's time to do something different.

Other countries are fascinated with gun toting Americans and believe that We the people control the government. All of those little countries around the world that the media is trying to compare to us, you can't drive five hundred miles without a passport, speaking another language and your human rights are severely restricted across every border.

Why can't we just end this argument by asking Americans to vote on the 2nd Amendment? The majority vote wins. Then enforce the Constitution according to the people today.

Challenge Nineteen

In response to the increased coverage of accidental shootings, Niggas Ltd. is introducing: The Wannabe. The Wannabe is a pistol that appears to be something it's not. The Wannabe is not a real pistol, but they resemble some of the most well-known handguns available. The Wannabe is designed for individuals who don't want to carry a weapon to hurt anyone but would like a passive-aggressive deterrent. Trained law enforcement officers, criminals, and news reporters apparently can't distinguish the difference between firearms and household items like cell phones or hand drills. Because the Wannabe looks like a real weapon, no one will challenge their potential. Made of technologically advanced and traditional gun making materials, Wannabe's are easy to find, and you never have to get them loaded.

The I Wannabe is wirelessly connected to your smart phone, recording your view of events and virtual hit zones with the weapons integrated camera. The Tech Wannabe is almost indistinguishable from a modern polymer semi-automatic pistol and fires only a red lazar pointer like those used on presentation pointer. The Wannabe Special, this little pistol gets everyone's attention. It is fully customizable with all the bling from sparkling diamond sights to glittering gold hand grips. It fires only a strong scented stream of traceable dye like department store anti-theft devices and automatically sends a call to the police. Wannabes are so good at looking like real firearms that law enforcement agencies have listed them as dangerous to the safety of police officers. Being seen in public with a Wannabe can result in your personal injury or death. Wannabes are legal in all 50 states.

Please let me protect myself!

I'm not proposing that any US citizen be forced to carry a weapon for any reason. I'm not proposing an end to background checks for the purchase of firearms. But shouldn't the background check for purchase of firearms be enough to permit possession of those arms for lawful use? The separate request for a concealed carry license is nothing more than a revenue generator and is mostly denied to African Americans and people living in urban areas. I am not advocating indiscriminately arming everyone. Isn't it every citizen's right to be prepared to protect and defend ourselves, family, property, each other, and the country? You can choose not to be armed. The right to choose is one of the things that make us free. People need firearms education and practical training for the safety of the country. Choosing to be armed will not solve our problems. Neighbors who do not respect each other cannot be expected to trust each other or defend a common objective even when there are real benefits for the whole community.

Private businesses, public institutions, and individuals can continue to ban weapons from their property, police and criminals will continue to ignore these rules. I'm not looking to roam the streets to stop bad people from doing drive-by shootings or issue traffic citations. I'm not requesting permission to apprehend or confront criminals. I'm not trying to interfere with police investigations or activities. Law enforcement agencies can continue to do what they do best; respond after a crime has been reported. I'm not trying to convert anyone's soul or send them to meet their maker. I want the same rights that the Civil Rights Movement demanded yesterday that still has not been realized by African Americans today. The opportunity to enjoy every freedom guaranteed to every citizen in accordance with the US Constitution.

A citizen involved in a road-rage incident, shot and killed one occupant of the other vehicle and wounded a passenger. Prior to the incident escalation to violence, the citizen attempted to mitigate the situation by identifying himself as an off-duty police officer and offered his official identification to the occupants of the other vehicle involve. The two occupants of the other vehicle refused to hold their position at their vehicle and advanced on the citizen with apparent hostile intent. The citizen drew his firearm and fired on the advancing individuals in defense of his family and fear for his life. The driver was pronounced dead at the scene and the other individual was found critically wounded outside of their vehicle when police arrived. It seems reasonable that this citizen acted in self-defense. Considering the citizen was not acting in any official capacity at the time. He couldn't be sure if this was a random incident of road-rage or retaliation for some current or past law enforcement activity. You see if you had the same opportunity to defend yourself, incidents like this one would be rare for everyone. Most Americans don't go looking for trouble. The bad guys don't always wear masks. Sometimes they look just like good guys offering protection for a price. We should not be arming the rest of the world and disarming Americans at the same time for public safety. Diplomacy and democracy work when people are willing, and the outcome is a benefit to everyone involved.

Conflicts can be avoided or resolved when neighbors respect each other, and they agree on the rules without threat of force or violence. Your neighbors know you, your children, your friends, and your habits. Neighbors watch each other. When something is out of place in your yard, talk to your neighbors about it. When you can't talk to your neighbors, call the police. Then protect yourself from them. This commercial was brought to you by people trying to present an alternate reality to you. Atrocities against humanity like homelessness, starvation, rape, genocide, human trafficking, slavery, and government involved murder must be confronted as weapons of terror. The government/police can't always get there in time to save you. The defenseless people are always at the mercy of those planning to do harm and witnessed by those unable or afraid to do something about it.

We continue to build prisons to contain the people we're supposed to be afraid of. Individuals who have willingly broken our social contract and cannot be trusted to not harm others if permitted to freely engage with society. And we continue to manufacture laws to keep our prisons full of people that we know, our sons, fathers, brothers, sisters, mothers and daughters. Millions of capable people are forced into poverty by a system that seems to only serve those of us who have the most. Like hoarders they can never have too much of anything, regardless of how much it costs or how little others may have. Why can't our prisons be converted into human care centers and the guards turned into caretakers? These facilities would still be full of unwanted people but with each individual having the opportunity for change.

I don't know any African Americans that can say they feel safe everywhere they go in America. We encourage our youth to travel in pairs, never alone and avoid contact with strangers, especially the police. We teach them the respectful cooperative protocol of behavior for encounters with law enforcement (the Talk). And still, they're susceptible to attacks from groups of other people or armed police officers. Adults are subjected to the same threats as our youth as we try to avoid negative contact with predators, criminals or police, perpetuating a culture of fear. Our elderly population has been terrorized into perpetual anxiety as a result of our toxic public environment condition.

Gun control advocates are trying to address this growing concern. This is not a war between the races, it's a class and power struggle and I don't want to be collateral damage. Survival instincts for humans are predatory and defenseless people will suffer. We've seen this happen all over the world. That was the unique experiment to create a country where everyone is treated equally. But that has never been the truth for African Americans. The denial of the right to self-defense continues to happen nationwide as the government tries to control a problem that doesn't exist. Ask yourself: Do you feel safe with the police? If the answer is yes, then you must be someone special. Some people want you to believe that you are somehow more dead if you have been killed by someone other than the police. The police want you to trust your life to someone who can't be with you all of the time.

There should be an outcry for gun safety training in all public schools. We provide training for other accident prevention programs such as driver's education and family planning. Which one of these things is more certain to result in death from a lack of education, careless behavior, and access to something that than can cause harm to others: guns, cars, or sex?

If America is going to be attacked, it is not going to be just from the air or on computers. It will be on the ground face to face like every conflict we've withdrawn from since the end of WWII. You can see how far we've come. African Americans are last on every positive American society index and first on every negative index in our consciousness. Building a coalition takes time and we've had more than a hundred years. There's a reason that we're still consciously at the bottom and it's not that we haven't proven ourselves with blood and brains. Making, selling and using firearms for protection, law enforcement, and profit is an evil idea. But don't expect the bad guys or the good guys to show up without them.

For everything forbidden there are challenges to the restriction and something worth fighting for from all perspectives. We should never forget that well-trained, armed, uniformed police officers hunted us like animals for individuals and a government that classified us as less than human. It was written into law and carried out by patriotic citizens. I can't help that so many of my people have been hypnotized into unconsciousness by technology and celebrities. Those people who experienced the searing sting of water from fire hoses and the vicious assaults by purposely trained dogs used by the police to deny us what is guaranteed to all Americans their sacrifices should not be in vain. Their children, grandchildren, and great grandchildren are being subjected to physical abuse and chemical warfare by law enforcement for public safety. Let's not forget the deadly encounters with lynch mobs of armed, misguided citizens who used disenfranchisement, deformation, intimidation, torcher and murder to deny us what is guaranteed to all Americans. This was happening while America was taking African American men from every state, even states where they couldn't vote, to fight wars that didn't benefit us. This is not to ignore the lives and contributions of African American women. However, like other Americans, African American women volunteered to participate in the war effort. African American men were drafted into action or imprisoned for refusing forced military service during the conflict of WWII.

My fellow Americans, if you don't want to be armed, please don't arm yourself. You are guaranteed the same level of assistance and protection by law enforcement as armed law-abiding citizens when trouble fines you. We, African Americans surrender our rights too easily out of fear, while everyone else fights for theirs. Guns and drugs are not the only source of problems for impoverished areas of America. Crime is big business no matter which way you fit into the equation. If the shoes of America are held on with colorful laces, African Americans must be the sole of America's shoes. Because we have been walked on for so long that we have forgotten how the sole can make the entire body uncomfortable. But America can't just take us off and throw us away.

Gun control is not about the tools we call guns. This is about control of Americans by artificially created fear of everything and everyone. Why? The criminals, police, and government don't have to worry about African American veterans being a threat because we don't manufacture any weapons. Where the majority of us live, possession of a firearm without the local government's permission is a felony with mandatory prison sentences and forfeiture of voting and other rights.

American corporations and banking institutions may have global interests, but most Americans have never been outside of the borders of the United States and maybe not even the states where they were born. These broader concepts of American interests abroad have not fared so well for people where I live. Small manufactures have been forced out of business by government oversight and cheap overseas manufacturing costs. Big manufactures have labor intensive and environmental polluting services performed outside of our boarders, taking our security and manufacturing capabilities away from Americans who are expected to buy imported items. Cheaper products at what cost! We don't have to buy this stuff. During the demand for independence, the people of India chose to wear only homemade clothes to develop a conscious idea of self-determination. Mass cooperation ended the British occupation and economic control of India. Martin Luther King Jr. asked the black people of Montgomery, Alabama to boycott the city's mass transit system to demonstrate the power of our money. Collective efforts ended public access discrimination nationwide. Where I live, most people have to leave their home unprotected because they travel long distances to work. And we travel in fear, including fear of our spouses, children, neighbors, strangers, and the authorities. No one wants an encounter with law enforcement personnel even when you call them. These encounters can be stressful and costly, if not deadly. There has been no outcry from the corporate media, our elected officials, the clergy, or peaceful citizens to disarm the police. With all of the new gun control laws enacted this year, none imposed firearm restrictions on police. The police record of misuse of firearms, excessive force, shooting unarmed people, untold firearm accidents and lost or unaccountable firearms is nothing to be proud of or feel safe with. Demilitarize our local police. I'm not saying that they can't have military stuff. They just can't use it in our cities. Situations that require military tactics and equipment should be addressed by the military and not civilian police departments.

America has to have some strait talk with itself regarding what it means to be American. Let's stop allowing ourselves to profess profound connection to another country (Hyphenated-Americans), flying the old countries flags and having ethnic heritage parades. All of these competing loyalties is not making this country better. A common cause brings people together just like a common enemy. I'm American, but when you look at me, you may be thinking that I should know my place. I do. I'm equal to you.

But today I just want to be able to protect and defend myself. If I use a weapon, it will not be by accident. The decision will be mine, not the weapons. Let the jury decide if I violated your rights, but simple possession of a firearm should not be a crime. And those "Red Flag" laws that are being introduced across the country should raise a huge red flag to all free Americans.

Challenge Twenty

As a result of the California Assault Weapon Ban, featureless rifles are being considered across the country. In response to the need for quality rifles that meet the AWB requirement, Niggas Ltd., is introducing an extremely modular rifle that is designed to be 50 states compliant. It will be called: The Black. Shooting enthusiasts are already looking for an accurate and safe alternative to permanently modifying their existing AR and AK platform rifles that can be easily converted in a modular design which can be configured to any state's legal requirements without permanently affecting the operational safety of the weapon.

The Black is available in two unique basic configurations. The Black Liberal: Is fully California AWB compliant, fixed non-adjustable front and rear sights, fixed non-adjustable stock, fix non-detachable small capacity ammunition magazine, standard rifle grip, standard rifle barrel stocks, no flash suppressor or muzzle brakes, and none of the other evil feature that make modern tactical style weapons operationally efficient. It does come with our patented breech block speed loader. The Black Conservative: Is a shooters rifle chocked full of features and accessories to customize your rifle to your exacting standards. It is 43 state compliant with adjustable stock, tool less detachable variable capacity magazines, accessory attachment rail for adding sights, scopes, lasers, flashlights, and a threaded barrel designed for flash suppressors, muzzle brakes, and sound suppressors. The Black Liberal is chambered for the 5.56 NATO round used in the AR-15 style rifles. The Black Conservative is available in a variety of calibers from the 7.62 NATO round used in the AK-47 style rifles to .50 Cal. used in precision sniper style rifle applications. Both will be made of technologically advanced composite plastics and traditional gun making materials.

Like all Niggas Ltd. firearms, the Black Liberal and the Black Conservative are cheap to own, easy to control, easy to get loaded, and very adaptable. Both models are built on a standard but flexible AR platform. With just a few screws their appearance can be changed without changing their function, lethality or impact on public safety, law enforcement, or crime. The basic rifles are indistinguishable from each other, but the Black Conservative comes with a large capacity magazine for use in places where the Black Liberal is not desired. Niggas Ltd. guaranties you will not be able to tell the difference in accuracy of either the Black Liberal or Conservative by looking at them. They both are American made to hit whatever subject you target with lethal consequences. Consider owning a Black Liberal or Black Conservative to protect you, your family, and your rights when lives are being threatened.

Everybody Knows

I'm not trying to convince you of anything. Everybody knows that African Americans don't manufacture any firearms. Everybody knows that where most African Americans live, possession of a firearm is illegal. Everybody knows that joblessness, poverty, and crime, is highest in African American communities. Everybody knows that most of the social issues that plague African Americans can be solved. So, why aren't they? I don't believe that we need other people to address these issues for us. We serve this country with our lives. We graduated from the best universities with honors. We fill up America's military and prisons with our children for reasons that defy logic. Why are we still waiting for a messiah to save us? Designing, manufacturing, selling, and possessing firearms can be part of the answer for all of the issues affecting African American communities.

Challenge Twenty-One

In response to the increased coverage of accidental shootings by law enforcement officers, Niggas Ltd. is introducing: The Clergy. The Clergy is a device installed in all police cars which will be able to call your cell phone or in-vehicle satellite based wireless device when being stopped by the police in a vehicle. During traffic stops the occupants of both vehicles would have a safer environment to discuss reasons for the stop and provide a means for electronic acknowledgement of the incident. This would reduce the incidence of negative encounters between the police and the public. If necessary, citations can be issued, argued, and paid via a downloadable app. The Clergy is a technologically advanced cellular communication device with dominant wireless connectivity. It can reduce dangerous interactions between police and the public during routine traffic stops. Touch and voice activated response to law enforcement instructions from the safety of your vehicle. Do you agree with the reason for this stop? Press one. If not, press two and keep your hands where the officer can see them. The Clergy will be available in a variety of applications: The Preacher with invisible source control, the Rabbi with duplicate video recording, the Mullah with remote vehicle cutoff for law enforcement officers, the Priest with hands-free voice control, and the TV Evangelist with built-in webcam for real time sharing for a small donation. The Clergy will deliver the word to reduce the risk of dangerous situations for both the police and the public. Listen to the Clergy and stay out of hell.

What we can do today

At the time of the Civil War, firearm manufactures didn't have computers, 3D printers or Negros that had graduated from any university. But these people were able to supply two armies and the world with firearm designs that are still in production today. I'm sure that some smart Negros can put their heads together and do this. If not, someone else will make and sell those weapons to us.

Challenge Twenty-Two

Niggas Ltd. continues to introduce you to opportunities for businesses perfectly suited for blighted urban areas. Niggas Ltd. currently is looking for African American scientists, engineers, entrepreneurs, investors, and sponsors for its latest product and venture. An all-electric Race car called: The Dream. If successful, the Dream could be developed into an affordable vehicle for all Americans. The Dream could be designed, developed, and manufactured in an abandoned property near you. It will take tremendous amount of work, courage, and sacrifice to realize the Dream. All-electric Formula One style race car designed to compete against all other all-electric race cars around the world. As the world becomes more conscious of human impact on the health of our planet, the need for alternative energy for personal transportation is essential. All-electric cars are a part of the solution.

The Dream will be constructed of carbon fiber, aluminum, titanium body and chassis components. It will be all-wheel drive with independent computer-controlled motors. It will have the most advanced battery charging system. It will be capable of charging the batteries from any available power source including sunlight, streetlights, conventional charging stations, and kinetic regeneration to power the Dream for an unlimited driving experience. The Dream race car will be the test platform for development of practical transportation for everyone. The unique charging system which relies on available, useable, renewable, sustainable energy sources will make the Dream affordable and recyclable. Niggas Ltd. wants you to pull the race card and help realize the Dream. Then you too can say: I have a Dream!

Conclusion

African Americans own entertainment and sports franchises producing and promoting athletes and entertainers, known around the world. There are African American billionaires. We see the evidence of their prosperity and privilege on TV, in magazines, and on our social media. We have been presidential contenders, President, Vice President and Secretary of Defense. But we don't manufacture any firearms anywhere. If you cannot defend yourself, you will be at the mercy of everyone else. This is a challenge for all African American graduates of the best universities on earth, and all veterans that have selflessly served in our country in its armed forces. This is a challenge for you to form collectives and co-operatives to develop, manufacture, distribute and sell firearms and related products for personal protection and police service. The manufacturing of firearms is one of the most profitable enterprises on earth. It should also be clear to everyone that buying, selling, collecting and trading weapons are also extremely lucrative enterprises. Using firearms for crime and law enforcement is also extremely profitable and African Americans should not just be consumers and victims of these products that make so much money.

African Americans, Colored people, Negro, dark skin, mulatto, biracial, people of color, Niggers, Blacks, sisters, brothers, and others have never been safe from the army, the police, elected officials, other Americans or each other in America. The right to be armed is not an exclusive issue for African Americans, as nothing in this country is ever about just one thing. For every action there is a reaction. Look around the world, gangs and governments are fighting for the control of defenseless people and their resources everywhere.

African American military service members and veterans, you have given a blood oath to serve and protect this country from all enemies foreign and domestic with your life. That oath did not expire with your discharge from military service. As a veteran, I don't believe that any state has the authority to prohibit veterans from being armed at all times just like any police officer without State or local law enforcement approval. Most African Americans live in or near major metropolitan areas where unemployment and crime are higher than the national average. Police presence is overwhelming and your right to defend yourself is severely restricted for their safety. What about yours?

We graduate doctors, scientists, engineers, teachers, reporters, lawyers, artists and great thinkers from the best universities in the world and have given birth to generals commanding the most powerful military force on earth. But African Americans don't manufacture any firearms anywhere on earth. Among us are countless philosophers, entrepreneurs, activists, preachers, neighbors, prisoners, police officers, teachers, convicts and politicians, but we don't manufacture any firearms or related products. All of the firearms confiscated from African Americans in connected with violations of the law or during gun buyback programs, used by all law enforcement agencies, the military and citizens everywhere are manufactured outside of our communities and control.

It should be clear to you now that when you cannot protect or defend yourself people will take advantage of you, hurt you, and kill you for their beliefs and for control over you. I hope that you discovered a variety of firearms and self-defense related products in these pages that should be produced by African Americans today. These challenges are yours for the taking. According to the Constitution the states have no authority to deny any inalienable rights to Americans. That includes your right to keep and bear arms. All of these challenges can be developed today without any unnecessary burden on the American people or economy. The challenges are presented with politically incorrect and impolite product names, titles, and descriptions to remind us of the injustices suffered by our ancestors and to desensitize us to the only language that we know, American.

Niggas Ltd. has decided to adopt a new name for the company. Niggas Ltd. is now Never Again. African Americans are still rotting in jail and rotting on the street like discarded vegetables waiting for disposal. We still manufacture less than any other clearly identifiable people in America. Not all of us are suffering financially. But that doesn't make us equal. Some corporate media personalities said that everything that happens in America today is blamed on the institution of slavery. However, I would argue that the grievances arise from what has happened since the practice of slavery ended. Remember, African Americans are the only US citizens emancipated from property (chattel) to some level of citizenship. That gives us a unique status in the discussion of American freedom. We want to be able to walk outdoors without fear of other human beings, no matter what your color, ethnicity, national origin, age, religion, political beliefs, profession, sexual orientation or social identification is in America. We also want to engage in meaningful endeavors to provide for ourselves and contribute to the civil and economic success of our communities through collective effort and mass participation. Until then, we're all living in a hostile and oppressive environment. Niggas Ltd. new name is a statement of where we're going as a company and community. Never Again is not only our name, but also our philosophy for the future. Freedom is dangerous.

www.ingramcontent.com/pod-product-compliance
Lightning Source LLC
Chambersburg PA
CBHW060416310726
48976CB00003B/1075